To my Friends and Family,

You are the inspiration for my characters. Thank you for pushing me to finish; otherwise, it may never have been completed! I am forever grateful for your encouragement and support.

Part 1

Confessions

Tamina

I never really had a normal life. My mom and dad died when I was just a baby and I was sent to live with my Aunt Bea. She pitied me; at least I think it was pity. Maybe she just didn't like me? Oh, whatever!

To get me out of the way she sent me to these camps, which became my free-time hobbies. Continuing throughout summers I had to endure Gymnastics, Fencing, Karate, and Sailing. The one I enjoyed the most was sailing. I felt like I belonged on the water and standing at the helm gave me a sort of power I could never quite understand.

When Aunt Bea died I was sent to an orphanage. I felt abandoned because I was forced to leave the only friends I had known, the only kids my age that understood me. I became an outcast at my new school, but then again it was full of kids that had everything handed to them on a silver platter since they were born.

I guess Miss. Cove was the only one who understood me. She was a hyper and eccentric 32 year old who ran the orphanage. She was the only family I felt I had left.

My eyelids started to fall over my eyes, and I constantly had to pinch myself to stay awake. It was the last day of school, and I honestly didn't see the point of stuffing our heads with more useless knowledge that we would forget within the first week of summer vacation.

The last bell rang, waking me up, and sending a cheer through the class. I stuffed my book into my bag, and bolted out of the classroom. Standing a safe distance away from my locker, I watched Caleb and his cronies pull away from my locker, all laughing and whispering to each other. I waited for them to clear away before going towards it. I tentatively pressed my fingers to the lock and spun the dial. It opened with a soft click. I took the lock off, and shoved it into my bag. Opening the door, a note fluttered to my feet. It was written on a bright yellow Sticky-Note. I rolled my eyes, and crumpled the note in my hand.

God, I wanted to beat the crap out of him!

I emptied my locker, slamming my door shut, and I ran into Jake, my best friend.

"Sorry, I didn't see you," I said catching his arm so he wouldn't tumble to the ground. I looked at him.

"S'Okay Tam." He looked at Caleb and his cronies who were laughing and pointing at me. I let go of his arm. "What they say this time?" Jake asked.

"That I was an ugly geek." I glared at them.

"Just ignore them. Hey, I gotta go. See you sometime this summer right?" he asked quickly.

I nodded, "bye."

He winked at me then ran off, his dirty blonde hair bouncing as he ran. It made me laugh a little.

Taking a deep breath, I walked over to Caleb.

"What do you want?" he asked, his deep brown eyes looking at me with amusement.

"I want to know what your problem is," I demanded.

"You should know that troll face. You're the

problem!" one of Caleb's cronies spoke up.

"Yeah, I know. I just want to hear why I'm troll face, and why you hate me."

Caleb looked at me and I found myself staring face-to-face with a guy I had known since grade 2. Someone who used to be a friend.

"You protect the geeks, and when you do that you get to reap the consequences."

"Those are fancy words for someone who probably doesn't even know what they mean," I snapped.

His face flashed with anger, and I could see the tiny wheels spinning in his head trying to figure out a good comeback.

"All right, I'm done with this conversation. Now why don't you go to the cafeteria and fetch me a sandwich. That's all women are good for," Caleb said smugly.

Really? That's the best he could do? I thought to myself.

"Yeah, can I have a massage?" asked another one of his cronies.

"Ewe! No! I wouldn't let troll face touch me, or any of my stuff. She might be contagious!" Jessica screeched from behind me.

I'm done! Lord, please forgive me!

I punched Caleb hard in the face, turned around and slapped Jessica, then exited the high school. I was walking through the campus when I heard the harsh words of the vice principal, Mr. Stellar, announce over the PA system, "Tamina Jackson, please make your way down to the principal's office. He would like to have a word with you."

I turned on my heel and made my way towards the large gray building in the middle of the campus. The only times I was called down to the office was when I was falsely accused of doing something, or when I was actually sticking up for my friends.

I walked back into the main building, which was a big grey box of sorts with about a dozen windows all over the walls. Other than the bulky steel door that was splattered with graffiti and box shaped bushes surrounding the entire building, there was nothing colorful about the main building.

A shiver ran down my spine as I heaved open the metal door and slid inside. I walked down the hallways with my eyes trained on the floor. I looked up just in time to avoid running into the Principal's door. I took a deep breath. Even though I shouldn't have been nervous, I was. I turned the doorknob and stepped inside to find Mr. Davis, leaning so that his back was up against his desk, facing away from me.

"Principal Davis," I said stepping forward and sitting down in a chair.

"Ah, Tamina, have a seat," Mr. Davis said. "Now we have to discuss an important matter. You have always been an ideal student and role model to other students, but you seem to be getting into as much, and maybe even more trouble than the bullies are! I am truly very sorry to say this, but you are being transferred to a school in Victoria for troubled kids."

I raised an eyebrow at him and laughed. "There is no school in Victoria for troubled kids. You're making that up," I said nervously.

"Really, and how would you know that young lady?" he asked, turning his head to the side slightly.

"Because we live in Victoria," I answered.

"Right. Well, you shouldn't talk back Miss. Jackson," Mr. Davis said.

"Wait a second. I know what this is all about," I interrupted.

"Really? Mind telling me what that is?" he questioned.

"You just want to get rid of me because I'm an orphan. I'm an embarrassment to the school, and you're trying to protect its perfect record."

"Yes, that is exactly it. But I'm afraid you're missing one tiny, little detail. You're not an orphan Tamina."

"Principal Davis. You wanted to see me sir?" someone asked from behind me. I turned my head and saw my best friend Jake standing in the doorway.

Jake

I was weird. The Greek Mythology geek. You know what that got me? Humiliation. Embarrassment. Worst of all, ignored and out casted.

Greek Mythology was the only thing I excelled at. I blame my parents. It was what each of them taught at separate Universities and they felt like sharing that knowledge with me.

Their favorite story was about the love between Poseidon and Amphitrite, the children they had, and the war that was almost waged over their eldest daughter. Amphitrite gave birth to Poseidon's three children, Triton-a Merman, and Rhode and Benthesikyme-the first Mermaid-Sirens. Triton went unmarried and lived to protect his home, his sisters and their spouses, and especially their children. Benthesikyme had seven children, three boys and four girls, becoming one of the most powerful women in the Ocean. Rhode had three children, a son named Ryder, and two twin daughters named after the royal jewels, Sapphire and Topaz. Rhode was Poseidon's favorite daughter, and when the girls were born, he granted Rhode three wishes. She wished them to be beautiful and talented, and let Poseidon bestow the third wish himself. He gave them great Power; some of his power over the earth, and ocean, and split it between the two girls. Sapphire became the Land Princess, and Topaz became the Ocean Princess. Three weeks after their birth, their underwater kingdom, was attacked and the girls were separated.

Topaz went to her opposite domain on land for her protection, and Sapphire stayed with her brother in the ocean. Sapphire and Ryder were raised together wondering where Topaz was, while Topaz never knew of her past.

To me that story was, well, just that, a story and nothing more than a myth. My parents would beg to differ. They believed it. They believed that Topaz lived with us now, not as an elderly woman, but as a young girl, a teenager, waiting for her future to be brought to her and her destiny placed in her hands to take it.

My parents had a way of making you believe what they were saying, like it was a matter of life or death.

I've lived in Victoria for four years (the longest I've ever been in a town); I have a small group of friends, my outcast friends. Each of them had something different about them that made them targeted by the popular kids. Then again, it was high school. In Grade nine you're branded for the rest of your high school career. Good luck!

There were seven outcasts in total, me included. Two girls and five boys. Carter, Dylan, Axel, Leonard, and me. We were the geeks. Computers, mythology, math, and science: you name it; we knew it. The girls however, we had no idea what they were doing. They were beautiful and best friends, but had the weirdest obsessions that made them outcasts. Skylark, well she voluntarily hung out with us, and was a smart aleck. She loved to stand at the top of an apartment building and drop water balloons on unsuspecting passers-by. Tamina however, was my best friend, and had the coolest hobbies. Hanging out with the guys and me, branded her as an outcast almost immediately.

I walked into the main building, and straight towards the principal's office. I opened the door. I saw Tamina, she snapped something quietly at the Principal and he replied just as silently. It was like they were whispering a secret and they didn't want anyone to discover it.

"Principal Davis, you wanted to see me sir?" I asked, clearing my throat for attention.

Tamina turned to me, her bright grey eyes shining. She swiped a lock of her fiery-orange hair behind her ear as she turned back to Mr. Davis.

"What do you mean? Of course I'm an orphan. I have lived in an orphanage ever since my Aunt Bea died," she said as she sat down, dazed with confusion.

Mr. Davis turned around and faced me for the first time since I entered his office. Except, it wasn't Mr. Davis, the principal. It was the vice principal, Mr. Stellar.

"Tamina, Your Mother made me promise to protect you. Your Grandfather made me promise to watch over you and bring you home when the time was right. To bring you back to your friends, where you could be properly trained for your role in your Kingdom. Please, I want to protect you. Your sister needs you, and I want to save your Kingdom. It belongs to you, Tamina. You are the Princess of the Ocean. In your Kingdom I'm known as Triton, and now is the time for you to come home," his voice pleaded, but his face showed no emotion.

My head whipped to look at the apparent Princess. My best friend. Tamina looked just as confused as I felt.

"What the hell is going on?" I blurted.

"You Jake Chase, know too much for your own good, and now need to be protected. I'm sorry but your coming with us too."

Tamina

I felt like laughing, and blurting out 'I'm not a Princess!' but I couldn't. I just had a feeling that deep down he was telling the truth, but I didn't want to believe it.

I stood up and scanned the room for a weapon, just incase the time came that I would need one. Then, I spotted the perfect one. A sword hanging suspended on the wall, just waiting for me to grab it. It was calling my name, begging for me to use it.

"You know Mr. Stellar, I mean Triton. I honestly think you're going crazy," I said trying to keep my voice steady. "You should really see a specialist. Hallucinating, making false accusations. I'm Tamina Jackson! I don't have a Kingdom. Happy now?"

"Tamina, Tamina, Tamina. I thought that you would have realized your true calling by now, but I was obviously wrong. I'm afraid that we can't wait any longer. In fact, we've been waiting too long already," he said snidely ignoring my own comment.

He unsheathed his sword from his hip and held it out in front of him.

"Come on Tamina, be reasonable. This is a one-ended fight. I have many people standing behind me who would like to take you home, and we can't do that without you listening. Please, I don't want to have to hurt you. I promised your Mother," Triton said sadly.

In a swift motion, I grabbed the sword from the

wall and stepped in front of Jake. "My Mother? She's dead! You never knew her! I will never come with you!" I said through gritted teeth. "I don't know you! I don't know what Kingdom your talking about! Why should I believe you?"

He narrowed his eyes and lunged at me, but I easily deflected his move with a karate kick to the gut and he doubled over. I quickly disarmed him and pinned him to the wall with my swords blade to his throat.

"Well done Tamina, you really are your Father's daughter," he said with a smirk on his face.

I whacked the side of his head with my sword's hilt and he sank unconsciously to the floor.

"I am no one's daughter," I spat out.

I threw the sword to the ground. Then, all of a sudden a rumbling sound came from the hall, sounding like a stampede. The monstrous footsteps came closer to us. I pulled Jake to the wall and in walked a very tall, muscular man that sent a shiver down my spine.

I tiptoed up behind him and kicked the back of his knees. He fell to the ground with a satisfying thud, but regained his balance in a matter of seconds. He threw a punch at me and I ducked quickly. I dropped into a sweeping kick and knocked his feet out from underneath him, a jerking pain shuddering through my shin. He fell over and this time knocked himself out by smashing his head on the floor.

"Not so tough now, are you?" I said bitterly. When the words escaped my mouth I wished I hadn't said them.

"Tamina, what in the world is going on?" Jake whispered from behind me.

"No idea Jake."

Suddenly, I felt someone watching me from behind. I turned slowly and saw two men standing in the door way, just as ugly and huge as the first.

The hand came forward and before I could react, he covered my mouth with a grimy hand. His hand gripped a chunk of my hair and pulled, making it feel as if my hair was being ripped out of my head by a train. I struggled against his grip, but couldn't break his hold.

The other man walked over to Jake and picked him up, throwing him over his shoulder like a sac of flour. The man holding me did the same, except he took a couple long strips of cloth and tied one over my mouth and the second around my wrists. He started walking and my head banged into the doorframe; making my vision go fuzzy and I let myself slip into unconsciousness.

* * * * * * * *

My eyes opened and I was on the floor of a van with Jake right beside me. I tried to sit up, but that motion awarded me a hard kick in the back making me reel with pain. I spat out the dirty sock shoved in my mouth.

"Where are you taking us?" I asked.

Then a familiar voice spoke up from the driver's seat. "Well, we need to speak to Miss. Cove about a few items that you'll need and then you Topaz, will be making a phone call," said the voice of Triton.

"Why? I already told you I don't have a Kingdom." I questioned, getting even more confused than I already was.

"Are you sure about that?" Ugly #1 scoffed.

I shifted a little on the floor, bracing myself for another kick that didn't come. I sat up, and brought my knees up to my chest. Lifting my arms over them, I hugged them tightly, resting my chin on my left knee.

"Tamina where are we going?" Jake whispered from beside me. He blinked his eyes fast, like he was holding back tears.

"To the orphanage I live at. To talk to Miss. Cove, the caretaker. I thought I could trust her. Guess I was wrong about that."

The van came to a hard stop and I lurched forward. I had to pull my arms from around my knees to stop myself from smashing my face into the floor. I pushed myself off of the ground, and landed on my butt again. I stretched out my legs. They were short; then again, I was short. I doubt I was going to grow anymore for the rest of my life, which made me short.

"Untie Topaz, leave the boy. He doesn't need to see this," Triton said.

"NO!" I said. The words slipping out of my mouth harsh, and demanding.

I turned to look at Triton while on my knees. I was looking into his eyes. "I'm not going if Jake doesn't come. Either he comes with us, or I don't leave."

He looked at me, shock barely registering on his face, but it was there.

He nodded at Ugly #2. "Take her."

I turned around as Ugly #2 shoved Jake to the side. Wrapping me around the waist, he picked me up slightly, throwing me over his shoulder and dragging me out of the van.

I was thrashing, digging my nails into his neck,

and kneeing his rock solid pectoral muscle. He dropped me on the ground. I looked at him confused, as he knelt down in front of me.

"Your Highness, forgive me. I am only following orders," he said, his voice quiet and slow.

"What orders?" I asked.

"I've been ordered not to tell. Sorry." He gave me a wink and a small smile as he got to his feet.

I gave a little huff, and walked away from him and straight into the faded pink house.

I took in a deep breath, the familiar scents of the house calming me. Baby powder, peaches, and apple pie. Then I was reminded of the fact that Miss. Cove, from the orphanage, may no longer be my friend, and that this may not be a safe place for me anymore.

"Go in Topaz," Triton said softly.

I rolled my eyes, and stepped through the doorway. The house was empty, which was a big difference from what I was used to because there were six babies, seven toddlers, and an eleven and twelve year old who lived here as well as myself. The place was usually loud and destroyed. Not now though. Now it was dead quiet and spotless. It sent a shiver up my spine.

Miss. Cove walked down the hallway. Her bubblegum pink hair glowed in the bright light of the hall, but she wasn't smiling. Not like she usually did. Now, she was wearing a fake one, one with the ends turned up a little and her lips pressed together.

"It's time?" she asked, her own silky voice sounding worn down and shaky.

Triton nodded beside me. "Yes, Abigail. It's time."

Abigail. I had never heard Miss. Cove's first

name before. Ever. It suited her; she began to look like an Abigail, instead of a Miss. I could imagine the teenage version of her. Not the 32 year old before me.

"Well, come on in then. Let's go to the living room. We'll be more comfortable in there," she gestured towards the door to our right. I knew where I was going, but they didn't.

I stumbled into the living room and took a seat in the soft recliner that I had claimed for myself when I first came here. As the oldest, I got first pick for everything.

Everyone seated themselves. All except for Miss. Cove, who leaned against the dining room table.

"Topaz, your Father is alive, but just barely," Triton said, through the awkward silence that had filled the room. He snapped his fingers and a small-scaled map of the Western Coast of B.C shone in front of us, made entirely out of water.

"You're Grandfather ordered your return recently. Miss. Cove and myself have kept watch over you these past years, and now it is time for you to return to your Kingdom. Right now we are here," he said pointing at a small red dot. It zoomed in to a bigger scale with a swish, like swishing mouthwash around in your mouth. "We need to get here." He swiped his hand across the map and it moved slowly to a blue dot that rested right in the middle of B.C. and New Zealand. It reminded me of Google Maps a little.

"Triton, I swear if you drop that Ocean Scan on the floor you're cleaning it up this time. The last time you bolted out of here and left me with the mess and I had babies to look after!" Miss. Cove said sternly, wagging her finger at him.

I held back laughter. It was humoring watching Triton getting told off by Miss. Cove. Then again, he's been telling me off since the beginning of high school so I guess now we're even.

"You know why I had to leave Abigail," he said rolling his eyes, and I saw a younger Triton, a teenager. I realized that even though he was my vice principal, he looked younger.

He shoved a hand in his pocket. "Now back to this," Triton gestured at the scan. "Your Father is there, he was recently captured as he went to visit your siblings, Sapphire and Ryder. Topaz when we get to this destination, you are going to have to get down there and get past the guards to get your Father out while we hold off the other defenses. We'll discuss more of the plan on the way there. We have three days, as we have to be back at Atlantis before your fifteenth birthday, or the Kingdom goes to the next in line, which is Jasper."

"Why are you calling me Topaz? My name's Tamina. It always has been and always will. What if I don't even want this Kingdom? My opinion hasn't really been a key factor in this equation. Who and under what circumstances says that I am even able to be the Queen of Atlantis? Which isn't even real, no?"

"It is real, very much so. Once you see it you will fall in love with it, I guarantee it. Topaz, you need to find and free your Father. You know in your heart that you have to. He's your Dad, you want to be the one to save him right?" asked Triton.

I closed my eyes and placed a finger to my temple and rubbing in a circle I took a deep breath. "Of course I want to be the one who saves him, but

I thought my parents were dead! I'll do it, but you are going to have to start explaining some things!"

He smiled at me, and I saw it again. All of a sudden he was younger and then he wasn't. Like a spell. "Good. Miss. Cove, that package please?"

She took a deep breath and made a clicking noise with her tongue. She got up and as she did so, flicked Triton in the ear. A grin spread across his face. Then SHE looked older, like in her seventies. Why was I seeing older and younger versions of people?

"Abby, you're slipping." Triton said, looking at his feet.

"As are you Triton," she said as she returned to her true age with the Bubblegum pink hair, white smile, blue-eyed Miss. Cove that I knew, not the elderly woman I saw moments before.

She walked over to the bookshelf and reached up to the top shelf with no problem. Unlike me, I still had a problem with reaching that shelf. She pulled down a thick book.

Setting it down on the coffee table in the middle of all the chairs, and just beneath the scan of the map, Miss. Cove opened the book. I could instantly see that it was hollowed out. There was a small black box in the middle, covered with a thin layer of velvet. She unclipped the latch and opened the lid of the box. Inside was a piece of yellowing paper folded many times, surrounding a leather necklace with three gems.

"This," she said taking out the paper and un-folding it, "is your Father's map of the seas. Only you will be able to read it, and only you will be able to figure out how."

She folded the map and set it back into the box.

"This was your Mother's necklace that she wore at her coronation. She had another one made for her wedding, with two Sapphires' and a Topaz. You never saw her without one of these on. They meant a great deal to her, and now, this one is yours."

Miss. Cove leaned forward and set the necklace around my neck. Clasping it on, it fit like a choker with the three gems resting on my collarbone.

"There are two Topaz gems and a Sapphire. If you were wondering," Triton spoke, "your real name is Topaz."

"These are yours, you will figure out who you are soon enough. We cannot help you in anyway. It is up to you to learn of your destiny. Now hurry, go. Night Devils approach the boundaries of the street. Go before they reach you." Miss. Cove smiled at me.

Hastily she got us up and out the door in less than a minute.

Ugly #1 and #2 were pulling me towards the Volkswagen. While Triton looked around hastily, sword unsheathed, ready to fight.

"Bye." I whispered, the word barely audible before they opened the side door of the van.

Jake

My head hit the plastic rim of the van door as it was shut and my vision started to get fuzzy. Everything started to spin, and the temptations to fall unconscious came. Then, everything went black.

****

I opened my eyes wide and rose to lean on my knees. I started to sway back and forth as I fought unconsciousness again. I threw all of my weight against the van door, slamming into the side with an impact that sent me flying back to the floor. I clamped my mouth shut and swallowed the yelp from the pain that shot up my arm.

I propped myself up on my elbow. With my hands still tied behind my back, I wasn't very comfortable. Out of the corner of my eye I spotted a knife lying hidden underneath the passenger seat. I turned slowly and just enough so that I could reach it.

As I brought it towards me I realized that if I were really going to use this, I would be cutting the rope with a razor sharp blade blind. I couldn't turn my neck far enough to have been able to see it.

I took a deep long breath and turned the blade in my hands so that the blade faced outwards, not towards me. I slipped the knife underneath of the rope so that I could feel the dull part of the blade against my spine. I closed my eyes and began sawing outwards, but the knife slipped and I felt the blade cut into my forearm. I bit my lip as I could feel a warm sticky substance, I guessed to have been blood, run down my arm. I regained my hold on the knives handle; gripping so hard I was sure I had white knuckles. I began sawing again and finally felt the rope loosen on my wrists and then break.

I carefully stuffed the knife back under the seat and took in the view of my arm. Just by looking at it I could tell that the cut was about an inch deep and I could feel the full extent of the pain.

I braced myself as I threw myself against the door, but when I did there was no door. I fell full-force through where the door should've been and collided with the sidewalk, my head banging on both a steel-toed boot and the concrete.

The collision sent me into another airy unconsciousness.

Tamina

I held tight to the box, containing my Dad's map. My Mom's necklace now fastened around my neck. Both of which belong to me and I would never let anyone take away from me.

Ugly #1 opened the door and Jake came tumbling out with a gash on his forearm. Knocking himself unconscious on Ugly #1's boot. I quickly leaned over and tucking the box under my arm, started to lift him just as Ugly #2 bent over and scooped his limp body up into his arms.

Ugly #2 took a step forward and set Jake into the back seat, putting the seatbelt carefully over Jakes lap. I pushed past the guy and collapsed beside Jake. Ugly #1 pushed an iPhone into my hand along with a number on a little slip of paper. I looked up at the dude as he said in a gruff voice, "dial it, you may get a little surprise by who answers."

I dialed the number and raised the iPhone to my ear.

"Hello?" a gruff voice answered quickly after two rings.

"Um, hi this is," I looked at Ugly #1 who gestured at me to go on, "Topaz."

"Topaz? Is this some kind of sick joke?" his voice tightened as he said my name with an infuriated tone.

"No! No, it's not. My name is really Topaz," I

said quickly.

"Oh my God! Topaz? Is that really you?" he asked his voice shaking.

"Yeah."

"Crap! Um, this is your brother. Your older brother, Ryder. We've never met but well, we have technically, but you were like 3 weeks old. You wouldn't remember me."

"Yeah, I wasn't told why we were separated, but that's okay. It's good to find out that I have a family," I said.

"Family? Weren't you with Aunt Bea?" he asked.

"Yeah. I was but she passed away," I answered. "Hey, how do you have a cellphone? I thought Atlantis was underwater?" I asked. Boy, am I confused!

He paused and I could hear him breathing raggedly.

"Um, sis, I don't live down there much anymore," he said slowly.

"Why not?" I asked.

"Well, uh, I don't trust them with anything after you were separated from us. They said it was for the best, but you're out of your element being on land. Who are you with?"

"Stellar."

"Who's that?"

"Oh right. Um, Triton?" I said correcting myself.

"Umm, Topaz that's probably not a good idea to tell him that name. Ryder blames me for you having to leave." Triton spoke up from the front.

"WHAT? Get him on the phone now!" Ryder yelled through the speaker.

I stretched my arm out and poked his shoulder.

"He wants to talk to you."

Triton gave me a pleading look through the rearview mirror and I shrugged. He took the phone from my hand and looked at me with his bright green eyes. He shook out his hair, and raised the phone to his ear.

"Hello?" He motioned for me to sit back down. I did. "I'm fine, how are you?"

I heard yelling from the phone all the way from the back. Triton pulled the phone away from his ear. "No, she's fine. I didn't kidnap her. Okay, maybe I did."

"Hey! What else was I supposed to do? She knocked me out." Triton raised a hand in the air, temporarily letting go of the steering wheel. We ventured down the gravel road, trees lining the parallel sides. It was like a thick forest, and the sun shining through the luscious green leaves turned the light green, and shining through the windows it tainted us it's color temporarily. "Which turn do I take again?"

Triton paused as Ryder answered. "Right, right. Okay I'm pulling up now."

"Watch your language Ryder! I may be family but I will not be spoken to with that tone!" Triton exclaimed.

"Family?" I asked.

Triton looked back at me. Meeting his eyes in the mirror, I could tell he had just said something he shouldn't have.

Jake

When I opened my eyes my head was throbbing. My eyes focused and I could see that the men were back and one was stooped over my forearm wrapping it in a bandage.

"Your lucky we have a first-aid kit, kid. Other wise you might have bled to death," he said softly as he tightened the cloth and pain shot through my arm. I winced but he wasn't even bothered by it.

"Thanks. I'm Jake. I don't know your name," I stated.

He looked up still tying a knot. "I know your name, kid. I'm Marvin and in case you were wondering, the redhead's up there."

I followed his finger to where it was pointing. I saw Tamina standing with a group of people heading towards her.

I instantly started to worry, but then images of Tamina floating in a wall of water, then sword fighting with a beautiful girl with dark brown eyes and dark hair, sent me into another headache.

I started to stand hoping that maybe my head was hurting because of sitting down for too long. I stood up and my knees buckled underneath of me. I almost fell but was caught by a pair of strong hands gripping my arm. Holding me up I heard Marvin's laugh for the first time.

I smiled and regained the strength in my legs. He let go and I was then standing on my own, being careful not to topple over.

"Thanks," I mumbled. I didn't want to appear weak, but it was very obvious that I was. I had this nerd factor that everyone in my class looked out for, and apparently I had a lot of it.

I started to walk away but the sound of a gun stopped me. Raising my hands to my head, I instantly turned around and saw the other guy standing with the gun in his hands, "Sorry, just making sure it was loaded."

I shook my head and started walking forward. It took a while and many breaks, but I managed to get to where they were standing.

"Jake!" Tamina exclaimed. "Your awake!"

"I'm alive too." I said brandishing my forearm.

"A great feat! Jake this is Thomas and Pamela," she said pointing at two of the three people standing beside her.

I nodded my head and the girl stuck out her hand for me to shake. "Great to meet you, Jake."

"Yeah, and same to you," I gulped.

Even in the little light, I could tell that Pamela was the beautiful girl fighting Tamina from my vision, or whatever it was I had a moment ago.

I shook her hand and let my eyes fall to my feet. I shot a glance at Tamina who looked like she was about to burst out laughing, which made my cheeks burn and I was certain that they went scarlet. I loathed being laughed at, in-fact, I still do.

"This is my big brother Ryder," Tamina said pointing to her right over at Ryder as he waved, shoving both hands into his pockets. He had green eyes, and a mop of black hair hung in his eyes. I didn't see any resemblance to Tamina.

I could feel eyes burning into my skull. I lifted my

eyes only to see Thomas' eyes boring into me. He sized me up, like he was figuring out how long would it take to knock me over, making me feel even more un-comfortable. I decided to shut my mouth about Pamela being the one from my vision.

"Thomas," said Tamina. "You look like your going to hurt someone. Are you okay?"

He nodded his head and looked towards Tamina, "what's he doing here?"

"Well, we were kind of kidnapped by Triton," she explained.

Tamina

I saw a group of kids come towards us. I recognized them, all of them from my childhood.

Bay, with her perfect glimmering white smile and deeply tanned skin. Her big hazel eyes shinning, and her chestnut brown hair bouncing around her as she walked.

Mallory, with her wired smile, light blue eyes, and pin-straight blonde hair that only moved slightly as though it were dead.

Jayden, with his dark brown hair, deep brown eyes, and brown skin.   Blake, with his white-blonde hair, pale blue almond shaped eyes, and yellow colored skin.

Sky, who lives up to her name, with sky blue eyes and the tips of her hair dyed neon blue.

Jack who still needed a haircut, with his hair pulled into a stub of a ponytail at the back of his head. He had dark brown eyes and white blonde hair, with lightly tanned skin.

"Oh my gosh! Tamina, how are you girl? Haven't seen you in like, forever!" Mallory spoke up in her annoying high-pitched southern lilt.

"I'm great Mal. What are you all doing here?" I asked.

"We hang out with Ryder every summer, he pays us to do the gardening, and sometimes, we just want to get away from our houses. He teaches us stuff sometimes. Showed us how to fence one summer. It's beautiful, really." Bay said speaking up. She came forward and gave me a hug and soon the others surrounded me, also giving me hugs. I could tell something was up.

I looked at Ryder over Jayden's shoulder as I gave him a hug. Ryder was grinning from ear to ear as he shrugged.

"All right, all right, break it up kids, intro's over. You're in the presence of royalty and I don't want my little sister injured," Ryder said getting in between Jayden and me. "They're going to help us find Dad. Topaz, you got the map?"

I nodded as everyone looked at each other in confusion. I laughed outright.

"My real name is Topaz, but don't worry I'm still going by Tamina."

I looked at Jake. He was looking around, but his eyes were mostly flicking back and forth from Pamela to Bay.

Bay on the other hand was looking right at him, with a stupid grin on her face. She looked at him like she was instantly in love, and ready to jump in front of a bullet to save his life.

I looked back at Jake, his softly muscled body, mesmerizing deep blue eyes, and when his hair got long enough, the ends curled. I always thought Jake was cute, like puppy dog cute, not at all gorgeous, or super model-like. I knew other girls thought of him like that, but they knew he was labeled a geek and that if anyone found out they liked him; they would be labeled geeks also. Bay, she was in love. I could tell by the way she was smiling, and through her eyes that she was in love. In love, with my best friend.

I rolled my eyes at her. She blushed and looked

to her feet.

The sun started to set a little. Pink spreading across the sky, blending with orange and some red. In a couple of hours, the sun would be gone. I heard the rushing sound of the ocean. I could smell the ocean and hear the water crashing into the rocks and I started to run.

"Tamina!" Thomas called after me.

I ran until I couldn't run anymore, for before me was a cliff, and at the bottom rocks rested on a sandy white beach. As I looked out further, there was the ocean. It was a beautiful, deep green color, reflecting the colors of the sunset onto its surface. I started to grin. I looked to my left to see if I could spot a way down and then to my right I saw it. I saw a trail, a ledge leading down to the sandy beach. I kicked off my flip-flops and left my friends at the top. The ocean was calling me. I could feel it. I could feel the ocean running through my veins, shaking my very presence, pulling my soul towards the crashing ocean. I ran down the ledge and through the sand, kicking it up behind me as I ran. I laughed. I walked to the edge of the ocean. The water rolling up onto the sand, and then pulling back. I stepped onto the moist sand. It was cold on my feet, but it felt good. I walked further into the water, until I was knee deep. I closed my eyes and put my hands down at my sides, feeling the ocean swirling around my legs, and the sand moving through my toes. I thought of it, of it's essence, moving, swirling in circles surrounding me almost like a hurricane.

"Topaz! Stop! Let go!" someone called ahead of me.

I opened my eyes, and I felt tired, drained. I was

even with the top of the cliff.

I looked down, and I saw exactly what I had imagined. I felt a hurricane of water lifting me into the air. I lost my focus and the hurricane dissipated, and I was suddenly 100 feet above the water. I started to fall, and then just before I hit the water, I was able to brace myself. I was caught in a wave of water the shape of a gigantic hand. It lifted me up, and set me up onto the cliff, then dissipated into a huge shower of mist that fell on top of me. I closed my eyes to escape the stinging spray of salt water.

I opened my eyes again, and wiped them. My arm was grabbed by an iron grip and I was hauled off the ground. I felt like a little kid again as I waited for a scolding, but it didn't come.

I looked over at Triton, who looked at me with concern. He looked younger, like he was Ryder's age, 18 at the most. My vision started to black out, his face covered with white blotches. I tried to hold onto my consciousness, but it slipped from my fingers.

Jake

I helped Triton lift Tamina up off the ground, and then he easily carried her in his arms. Ryder took off his sweater and draped it over her as she started to shiver.

Thomas was busy controlling his emotions. We walked behind Triton and Ryder who seemed to be arguing about something. I decided to run up with them, but stopped just shy of them, not wanting to totally eavesdrop. Okay yes, I ran up to eavesdrop on them!

"That was incredible! What do you think she could do when she's in the water Triton?" Ryder asked quickly.

"I don't know, but I'm sort of jealous. She's more powerful than I am. If Dad's going to give some of his power out to every one of his Grandchildren, I might as well have some kids of my own," Triton said, a hint of jealousy ringing in his voice.

"I have never seen anything like that! Imagine what she would be like-" Ryder said getting cut off.

"With Sapphire, that kind of power would get-"

"Atlantis attacked every other day. You ready for another security session?"

"You know, I was thinking of starting a family, or even spending more time with my own. If there's one thing I've learned in all the time I've had, it's you can never spend too much time with your family," Triton said.

"Say you do something valiant, would you take up

the immortal offering like Aunt Bea did?" asked Ryder.

"Look what good it did to her! The Under-lands have a weapon that they can use against us that can kill even the immortal. Benthesikyme, I mean your Aunt Bea, knew that and wanted to train Topaz on her own, like Rhode asked her to. I had to train you and Saph, I can't just leave my duties of protecting you three if I'm immortal, I would rather do all of that with my powers. I changed and looked old for almost a year to keep an eye on Topaz, then when Dad told me to get her out of there, I became younger. I was 30 when I started watching her, now I am 22. That can't be a co-incidence of my powers. They're using your Father, Matthew. They're sucking the immortality out of him, and by doing that making your Grandfather and I younger. You guys will stay the same." Triton tried explaining as we reached the door of a lighthouse looming over us.

We heard screaming behind us. I turned just as Pamela was scooped up into the arms of a huge green monster. I had a quick feeling that it wasn't the Hulk. Pamela screamed and struggled in his arms as he took his hand and grabbed her neck, twisting it. She went limp, and I knew she was dead. The monster took her body and threw her over the cliff edge from where he was standing, which was about twenty feet from the edge. He then turned and grabbed for Bay. She screamed and everyone scattered. Bay dropped to the ground, using her feet to kick at him. I ran towards the monster right before he grabbed her. Jumping on his back I covered his eyes with my hands. He grabbed at my hands trying to pull me off, but I quickly pushed my fingers into his eyeballs from where I was on his back. He screamed in pain and threw me off his back. I scrambled to my feet and pulled Bay up too. The monster was clutching his face, roaring in pain. I went over and quickly kicked where it counted. He bent over and moaned, groaning as I kicked him again in the groin. I grabbed Bay's hand and dragged her behind me towards the door to the lighthouse, where everyone had ran and watched the attack from the big bay window. I grasped the doorknob and began to open the door. Bay placed her hand on mine. I looked at our hands, and then I looked at Bay. She was beautiful. She wrapped her arms around my waist and pulled me into a hug.

"Thank you, you saved my life," she said into my chest.

"No problem," I said taking a deep breath as I put my arms around her.

"I owe you one," she whispered just barely. Then she let go.

With her warmth gone from me, I felt a tug in my stomach, and the urge to lean in and kiss her, but I didn't.

Tamina

I opened my eyes sleepily, and found I was in a dark room, lying in a soft bed that was covered in a large comforter, and surrounded by fluffy pillows. I pushed the cover off of me and sat up. A dizzying feeling overcame me and I gripped the side of the mattress. When the moment passed, I looked around. I recognized this room. This was where I lived until Aunt Bea died.

There was a floor length mirror that I looked at myself in. I had circles of exhaustion under my eyes. I was in a light pink nightgown, which I snarled at it. I utterly despised pink. On the bedside table was fresh clothing. I picked them up. It looked like a Greek chiton, with a braid for a belt. I sighed. If the only thing they had around here were dresses I am utterly screwed. I slid out of my nightgown letting it drop to the floor.

I grabbed the chiton from the bed, and pulled it over my head. Right as it dropped down and rested softly on my shoulders the door opened. In walked Bay and Mallory. They were wearing similar chitons, except theirs were more fitted, and they were a different color than my turquoise dress.

Bay's was a light pink, which had one strap that rested on her left shoulder. Her hair was in a braid with golden strands braided into it, making her hair look a little darker.

Mallory had her hair in a mass of curls resting

on top of her head, with little silver strands running through her hair. Her chiton had a thin stranded belt that wrapped around her stomach unevenly, with patches of her dress poking through the spaces. Her dress was a deep purple.

"You need help?" Bay asked.

I nodded, "please."

She laughed. Mallory stood back by the door, almost guarding it with a hand resting on her hip and gripping what looked like the metal handle of a knife. She closed the door.

The straps kept slipping off of my shoulders and I had to keep resetting them back.

"No, leave them. That's the way the dress fits. It drapes over the shoulder, in a loop. Not on the shoulder," Bay said slightly.

I let her tamper with the dress and tease my knotted hair into a braid while weaving golden strands throughout it. She then decided better and let my hair down again. Bay carefully curled it, with what I don't know. It turned back to my normal hair before I straightened it every morning before school. Then she wrapped a golden circlet around my head, resting it on my brow. She wrapped the gold belt around my stomach, in a similar way to Mallory's. Bay pulled out another band from the dresser drawer. It was an armband. She slid it up my arm until it stopped in the middle of my triceps. She stepped away, and bowed. I turned and looked in the mirror.

I don't know what Bay did, but I looked gorgeous. My hair flowed over my shoulders, and it was like the dress shrunk because it now fit me perfectly. I felt new. Like I fit in. Like I could fit into this lifestyle.

"Thank you Bay," I said not able to take my eyes off of myself in the mirror.

She laughed. "No problem. Um, when you went unconscious, you missed the attack. Pamela is dead."

I raised my hands to cover my mouth as a gasp escaped me. Tears sprung to my eyes and stung as I held them back. A black cloud came into the room. "Oh, no! Then Pamela would want us to do this."

Bay looked at her feet. "Do you think Jake likes me?" she asked so quickly, I hardly understood her.

"Yes. I think that with time, he will have the guts to tell you. I think that he likes you. He's just jealous," I said.

"Why would he be jealous?" Bay asked.

"Because you aren't his," I answered.

"I'm not any ones." She wrung out her hands.

"He definitely thinks that you are somebodies," I countered.

"Why would he?" Bay asked.

"I don't know. Jake has always had a habit of trying to protect the people he cares for. He tries to be their knight in shining armor," I started. "If he loves you, he won't be able to let you go. You could try to get rid of him, but it won't happen."

"You sound like you've been in that position," Bay said sadly.

"Jake would protect me, as I would protect him. We are like family. Nothing more than that. I guarantee, you go downstairs and he will instantly realize that he loves you, as you love him."

"You know that I have feelings for him?" Bay asked me.

"How could I miss it Bay?" I replied.

She blushed and looked at her feet.

"I will go down with Mallory. Wait a couple of seconds and then you may follow the stairs after me," Bay said, bowing and then turning the knob of the door, she walked out of the room.

Jake

Tamina sprung out of the door to the tower, but stopped dead in her tracks. She glared at the five men that were sitting with us and probably was thinking the absolute same thing that I thought when I first saw them. Who the hell were they? And could we trust them?

"This is Tamina?" asked Maurice.

Thomas nodded his head and looked at Tamina. His eyes almost immediately softened and I felt disgusted. He was in love with Tamina and everyone knew it. Tamina was still oblivious, as was Thomas to his own feelings.

I rolled my eyes as Tamina stepped forward slowly and as her eyes searched around the room for something. I knew that look only too well. She was looking for a weapon. I smirked, stopping myself from laughing as she spotted the gun on the kitchen counter. The gun Thomas himself had placed there.

As fast as lightning, she had the gun pointed and let off a shot. It went straight through the window with a loud crash just as another shot went whizzing past Tamina as she dodged it. Everyone dove under the table to hide from the rapid fire of bullets. I, however, sat there still amazed at what was going on. I watched as Tamina jumped up and front-flipped over two passing bullets and landed with two feet on the table. Another gunshot came and she did a round off backwards, the bullet just skimming her hair, while her dress gracefully moved with her. Tamina fired again and this time hit her target, which was standing just outside of the window.

I saw her take a deep breath and almost relax, until we heard another gunshot. Tamina pressed herself against the table and avoided being shot. The gunfire stopped and, as I always reacted very late, ducked down and hid under the table.

Then came another gunshot. The sound exploded as it came right for Maurice, who was standing behind the counter of the kitchen. Tamina pulled a knife from under her dress and threw it. The knife just clipped the end of the speeding bullet, knocking it off course and sending it into the wall.

Everyone emerged from the table at the same time, except for me, and almost immediately started talking about what had just happened.

Maurice speaks up. "You, Tamina. Just ... saved my life. I will be honored to give you Revenge, my ship, and in doing so, honor the Pirate Code."

Tamina looked at him, winded and confused.

"The Code says that if you save someone's life you own it. You own my life. If you need anything I will always be at your service." Maurice bowed from the waist, turned on his heel, and left with the other four who hastened to keep up.

We all stared at Tamina in disbelief, which left us all staring as she raised the gun to her mouth and blew above the barrel at the imaginary smoke. "Yep, that's right. I can shoot a gun!" she exclaimed smiling as she sat back down at the table.

"Okay, what is going on?" Tamina asked placing the gun in the center of the table.

"Thomas, you didn't tell her about the ND's? Are you freaking nuts?" Jack started yelling at Thomas.

"Those were two of them and they almost killed Tamina."

"I didn't want to. There was a reason," Thomas started.

"Didn't want to what? Scare me? I can assure you that I'm already scared out of my mind. People are going to die on this rescue mission and I'll bet you my life. What the heck is going on?" Tamina yelled at Jack and Thomas, making them both flinch.

"Listen, Topaz, Jack and Thomas are good kids that are trying to help you get your Father back. Those were Night Devils, and they want you dead. You, however, have the same training as they do and are one hundred times stronger and smarter. So, if you want your Father back alive, you might want to be a little less bossy and a little more strategic," Triton snapped leaning in towards Tamina.

I saw her nose wrinkle in disgust, and I couldn't help but agree to what he said. She slowly nodded her head and Triton backed up a little bit.

"Great, I'm going to need all the help I can get ... but I'm not letting anyone else risk they're lives for me," Tamina said silently, calming down.

"Other than us you mean," Jack said with humor in his voice.

"No," Tamina's voice was already loaded with sarcasm. "You guys can't come either, I'm too afraid that I'll have to babysit you guys."

We all busted out laughing, at what I don't know. Honestly, I was laughing at the idea of Tamina babysitting, because I knew that would be hilarious. She dislikes little kids. She never told me why, she just does, and she can't even take care of herself. Those poor children!

Tamina

"All right, I'm exhausted. Those awesome ninja moves have completely used up all of my energy and I wouldn't be surprised if I didn't make it up the stairs. So, where am I sleeping?" I asked.

Thomas chuckled, "your old room."

"Is that where I just slept? Again, I haven't been here for a couple of years so where in the world is my 'old room'?"

Exasperated, Thomas stood up, grabbed my wrist and pulled me up towards the staircase. "No, that was a different room. We had to put some bedding into your actual room. You were in Aunt Bea's room earlier. Do you want me to show you or do remember now?"

I smiled, "please."

I took a couple steps forward but my knees buckled and I lost my balance and fell backwards into Thomas' arms. Without saying anything, he scooped me up with my head in the crook of his arm and his other arm underneath my knees. I rested my head against his chest and heard his heart beating. It wasn't steady as it probably should've been. It was racing as if he was nervous being so close to me. We've been friends since we were kids and he's nervous around me? That seemed a little unreal.

I closed my eyes. I heard a door creak open and then shut again. I was being set onto the bed right in front of a huge bay window. My head hit the pillow, and I closed my eyes. I curled up into a ball and felt the blankets being pulled over me. I opened my eyes and started to say something just as Thomas put a finger to my lips and brushed strands of hair out of my face in a soothing way.

My eyes fluttered shut and I found myself falling asleep, very slowly. Thomas leaned over and kissed my forehead, making my stomach flutter.

A few seconds later, I heard the door shut and the staircase outside creak.

That was the first time that Thomas showed that he cared about me in another way other than like a sister. The first time he had ever shown affection for anything, and I saw a new part of Thomas that night. A part that let me know that he wasn't as hard-core as he led everyone to believe.

* * * * * * * *

The dream was definitely surreal. It was like the world had flooded over leaving absolutely no air to refuge in. The humans had morphed into a half-fish half-human species that became clear to me were Mermaids. There was a castle in the background, shining in all the colors of the rainbow as the sun reached it. Everyone was swimming around merrily, not noticing me in anyway, and making it easier to investigate. Soon, I figured out that I couldn't move. I looked around frantically, and that's when I saw her. She swam by me with a small silver circlet resting on her brow, and a necklace almost identical to mine, circled her neck with two Sapphires and a Topaz hanging from it. The things that startled me were; one, those were the exact gems on my necklace, and two; she looked exactly like me. I felt like I was looking straight into the mirror. I held my hand out and shouted a name.

"Sapphire!" The words escaped my lips and I couldn't retract them.

Her head turned towards me and a great big smile spread across her face as she came swimming towards me. As she swam forward, I went backwards farther away for her. She started to swim faster, but became too far away for me to see. We screamed each other's names and soon we could no longer see nor hear each other.

* * * * * * * *

I awoke with a shudder and found someone's arms wrapped tightly around me. I looked up and saw Thomas sitting on the side of my bed, looking down at me with his forehead crinkled with concern. I lost it. I started sobbing into his shoulder as he held me, rocking me back and forth, trying to calm me down.

"Tamina, it was just a nightmare. Nothings wrong, your safe. You're with me and I'll protect you, I promise. Your safe," he whispered softly into my ear through my hair. "I promise I will never let anything hurt you."

I choked on my own tears and pulled my head back from his shoulder. I wiped the tears from my eyes and took a deep breath.

"What time is it?" I asked.

"5:30," he answered around a yawn.

"Did I wake you up or something?" I asked.

"No, I was coming to wake you up. Triton thinks

that he doesn't want a huge commotion. It would gather too much attention from the neighbors. We should leave before they wake up."

I nodded my head and wiped my eyes again. He let go of me and I was overcome by a huge gust of cold air. I shivered and noticed that the window was wide open. I pointed at it and Thomas shrugged.

"I don't know what you were up to in here, but I happened to walk into the room just before you jumped out of that window," he said.

"Do you know where Sapphire is?" I asked.

"No, I don't," he answered.

He looked a little awkward standing there. I don't know if it was the whole bit of him being in my room or if he was overall just uncomfortable.

"Um ... there's some food downstairs in the kitchen we left out for you. The rest of us will be waiting at the dock, okay?"

"Can you wait for me, Thomas? I'll feel really awkward walking to the dock all by myself." It felt really unorthodox asking that question, though I really wouldn't have minded the company.

"Sure," he answered.

I smiled and he turned and left the room.

I stood up and noticed the pair of clothes laid out on the end of my bed. I peeled off the chiton I fell asleep in from yesterday and pulled on the T-shirt laid out for me. It wasn't exactly what I would wear, but it was clean and a shirt, and I was taught not to argue about what was given to me. I pulled it on over my head. The other piece of clothing I expected to see were jeans but no, they were shorts. I stood up and pulled the shorts on with much tugging and pulling. I did the button and the zipper up and had to sit back down to put on my socks and shoes.

When I was done I stood up and as I left the room my hand went to my neck where I found my necklace. Three gems. The same gems on Sapphire's circlet. As I quickly looked around the room I noticed the same gems in a picture hanging above my dresser. I fought off the urge to look back. I couldn't look back, because if I did I would just miss this place even more. I started down the stairs quickly with my hand trailing on the wall.

Jake

I walked onto the ship, pacing back and forth on the deck. I was worried. Thomas should've been back with Tamina already. What if a Night Devil jumped them? What am I talking about? Night Devils only attacked at night. Hence the name *Night* Devils. Then again, what was I worried about? Thomas would protect Tamina, even if it got him killed.

I walked up the stairs and over to the railing. I jumped up and hoisted my legs over the edge so they where dangling over the deck below. I watched the scenes below me. Blake and Jayden were readying the masts while Triton worked the ropes and a bunch of Triton's gang cleaned the ship up. I saw Thomas and Tamina walking from a distance, which made it hilarious for me because they had no idea I was watching them. They emerged from the trees and onto the dock. Without thinking I jumped off of the railing and onto the dock. Still wet from the fallen dew, I slipped and fell backwards. I braced myself for the impact, but it didn't come. Instead I felt a pair of hands grip my arm, pulling me to my feet. I leaned on the person to get a solid footing on the slippery wood.

"Are you okay? That was quite the fall," the voice said. It was smooth, and high with a slight hint of an accent.

"What do you mean? I just slipped on the wood," I said turning around.

I saw the girl who caught me. It was Jack's girlfriend,

Sky. She smiled.

"I meant the fall from the rail," she said trying not to laugh.

I shook my head, "Oh yeah, that fall. Yeah, no, I'm fine. I meant to do that," I said.

Sky laughed. "Sure you did."

"Is that an accent? I can't make out what it is," I asked.

"Yeah, it's French. I was born in Paris. Lived there for a while and then my Mom was transferred here to Victoria," she answered.

"Oh yeah? Cool. I was born in California. My family moves around once every year, lived almost everywhere," I said trying to mimic her accent.

She giggled. "You're going to need to work on that accent there. I know a couple of French guys that would beat you up for making fun of their accents."

"I'll keep that in mind," I said.

She smiled and walked away. I smiled back and turned to run over to Tamina and Thomas. I ran literally right into Jack.

I looked up at him and the smile on my face disappeared. "Jack, hi. Um, I was just going to see Tamina and Thomas. They, uh, are here. Yeah, so I'll go now."

I took a deep breath and walked away from him as he turned and watched me with hatred gleaming in his eyes.

"Jeez! Guys, where have you been? I've been worried that something grabbed you. You should know better than to disappear without telling someone," I exclaimed jokingly.

Thomas came over and put me into a headlock.

"Jake, you sound like my Mom. Relax!" he said.

Thomas let me go and I stumbled backwards. I put my fists up and came at him but Thomas stuck his hand up and blocked me from the head. His hands rested on my forehead as I was taking swings at him, failing miserably at making contact. Tamina laughed and grabbed Thomas' hands from my head, making me fall forward. I stuck my hands out just in time to avoid getting wood in the face.

I got up and said in my best high voice, "Thomas, dear, you've let your hair grow too long and look at the state of your shirt. My, my, you really need to have a bath young man."

Thomas laughed and threw a lazy punch at my head. I ducked.

"Jake, if you're looking for a fight, you'd be better off fighting Tamina than me. Just warning you." Thomas said to me pointing to Tamina over his shoulder, who was busy talking to Bay and Mallory. "Because you know, I'm so much better than her at fighting."

I saw Tamina turn around as she raised a finger to her lips. I held back a laugh, and Thomas just smiled like he was waiting for an assault to come ... and it did.

Tamina swept his feet out from underneath of him and she pounced on top of him. She flipped him over with her hands, pulling his arms behind his back. She pulled him up so that he looked like a seal on rocks.

"Who's better than whom at fighting?" she asked.

Thomas answered hoarsely, "you are."

She got up and off of him. Thomas stood up and bent over, his hands resting on his knees.

"I gotta stop letting her do that to me," Thomas whispered to me.

"You know Thomas, even if you did stop letting her do that, she probably still would," I laughed.

Thomas glared at me, which only made me laugh harder. Then all of a sudden, Thomas stood up straight and was no longer staring at me. He was looking at something behind me. I could tell we were moving but that wasn't it. I turned around to see Tamina talking to a guy in a uniform that had climbed aboard the 'Revenge.'

Tamina

"Excuse me little girl, where's your Mom or Dad?" the guy asked.

I put my hand on my chin in a thinking position and said, "Well, let's see. One's dead, and the other is lost at sea. So, neither of them are available to talk right now." I flashed him a smile.

"Amusing kid. Fine then, you want to play it like that? Who's the Captain of this fine pirate ship?" he asked.

"You're looking at her." My words were soaked in lemon juice.

"Yeah, right!" He chomped down on the piece of gum he was chewing. He, so thoughtfully was snapping it and bothering me at the same time, which I didn't think was possible. Obviously, I was wrong. "Listen kid, do you have a permit for this little search party?"

I glared at him, took at deep breath and said, "yes I do. I'm sorry for this whole misunderstanding."

He smiled, showing two rows of gleaming white teeth, which looked really weird with his dark brown skin. "Thanks kid. Can I see it?"

I shook my head. "You don't really need to."

I saw the ocean respond to my command. It listened. A huge wave came up, like a huge hand, a claw really, and grabbed the man from the waist. It pulled the man off of the boat and threw him away like a piece of trash. As the ocean subsided I saw the splash from where he landed. I waited, and then saw his head bobbing in the water a great distance away from us, but not that far from the docks.

I turned around and rubbed my hands together. "Well, that was fun."

Triton's mouth was hanging open like his jaw had been broken, making me laugh. I used the ocean and propelled us forward. We were now on our way, I guess.

Thomas and Jake stopped a couple feet away from me and both of them had shocked looks on their faces.

"How in the world did you do that?" Thomas asked.

"I'm the Ocean Princess," I said as a half-smile appeared on my face.

"What?" Jake asked.

"Believe me, I haven't known for that long, but I'm part mermaid. The next time I take a swim, I'll grow a tail. I'm hoping for purple, how 'bout you?" I asked.

Thomas gasped. "You can't be serious?"

"I am. Not really much I can do about it. What I've been told is that my Mother's name is Rhode and she was a Mermaid-Siren. I'm a Princess, my brother's a Prince, and Triton's my uncle." I paused. "Did I leave anything out?"

Triton shook his head beside Thomas and laid a hand on Thomas' shoulder, who looked confused.

"Come on kid. Lets go to the cellar and check the stocks, make sure we have enough for the journey," Triton said leading Thomas away and looking past his shoulder at me before disappearing down into the cellar. Triton shot daggers at me with his eyes. I immediately felt myself freeze. I rubbed my arms, hoping to make the gooseflesh disappear from them. I mouthed a sorry to Triton as he looked away, shaking his head.

"Life's not going to be the same, is it Ryder?" I asked.

"Tell me, when has life ever been the same? Isn't it ever changing?" Ryder responded.

I laughed, "I guess so. I meant it's not going to ... well, I guess I ... Did I have a future? In Atlantis?" I asked.

He looked at me sadly. "Yes. As did I, and Sapphire. You two were betrothed to Princes named Jasper and Cowan. You to Jasper, and Saph to Cowan. This promise made for you and Sapphire to marry Jasper and Cowan was nullified when you became separated from each other. I am presently engaged to their older half-sister Jordan."

My jaw dropped. I quickly closed my mouth, but then opened it again to say something. I must have ruined a lot of futures, I thought to myself.

Ryder started to walk away; he looked like he was almost considering trying to comfort me, then decided better of it. He walked away leaving me on my own. I turned to the Ocean.

"Sapphire, if you're out there. I hope you can hear me. I need you," I whispered.

The wind, grabbed ahold of my words like leaves fallen from a tree in the fall. I watched them catch in the ocean, and then slide across the waves and then they were gone. Gone to whisper into the ears of whoever could hear them.

Sapphire

I sat on my throne between Ryder's and my Grandfather's thrones, listening to another suitor. Another boy that wanted to be a man.

I needed my sister. She was supposed to be the Queen, not me. Not little, rebellious me. I needed her support, and the only person that understood me was my Grandfather. This job needed to be done or I would be forced to marry a stuck up Prince from the lower regions, because the betrothing had been broken.

I snuck a look over at Matt. He looked pained watching me up here, but the expression disappeared, and he gave me a little half smile. I returned it and looked back towards Lord Shark.

"Princess Sara, wit-" he started.

"Sapphire," I interrupted.

He was taken aback. I think it was because no one had the guts to talk back to him. I was definitely glad to be the first.

"Oh, yes. My apologies your highness," he said with a bow from the waist. I saw, as he bowed, a bald spot in the middle of his head. I snorted.

"My Lord, if you would excuse me. I would love to stay and see what your results are with the Princess, but unfortunately I have the duty to check on the soldiers," Lieutenant Conners exclaimed, bowed and then swam away. Lucky him, I thought to myself.

"Princess Selena, you will be under the safest protection, if anyone did decide to attack, you would be extremely safe." Lord Shark finished.

"My name is Sapphire!" I interrupted again. "The safest protection, really?" I questioned, pretending to be interested. I knew only too well that this was a total lie. Just last night I broke into his palace and know that right now, Lord Shark's own Lieutenant Conners is setting up for a raid on their own palace. They can't protect themselves. They can't even protect their own Lord.

"My Lord, I am pleased with your offerings, but my granddaughter will not need your protection," my Grandfather added.

"He couldn't protect me anyway Grandfather," I said slouching in my seat.

The Lord looked like a wounded puppy hearing my words and I almost felt sorry for him. "W-what do you mean your highness?" he stammered.

"I heard that there was a break-in at your palace only a night ago. Is this not true sire?" I asked.

"Yes, it is, but as far as I am concerned that is nothing you need to worry about," the Lord snapped.

"It is something to worry about if your intruder, was a girl." I rose from the throne. I planned on winning this argument and I stumbled forward. A loud hissing had filled the air around me and I could tell my Grandfather was affected as well. Matt came forward and caught me. He looked down at me, his face contorted with concern and the strain of holding me up.

"Its just Topaz, Sapphire. She entered the water, on a boat. Everything will be fine. I'm here," Matt whispered in my ear.

That's when I heard it, the noise. It was soft and came from every direction. Holding me against my will, I tried to fight it but the power was too strong. It echoed against the walls and didn't end. 'Sapphire, if you're out there. I hope you can hear me. I need you.'

The voice died down and I found my strength. My Grandfather looked as if a weight had been lifted off of his shoulders, he looked younger.

The Lord however, looked panic stricken and began to swim away faster than anything I had ever seen before. I laughed and pulled Matt closer to me. He didn't fight me as he wrapped his arms around me and lifted me off the ground, spinning me in a circle and then setting me down on my throne. With a hint of a smile on his face, he sunk back into the shadows.

I looked over at Grandfather, he was grinning. "You have my blessing to marry Matt you know," he said.

I raised my eyebrows at him, "What do you mean?" I asked with anticipation.

"Well, only if you were proposed to of course but, I know that you love Matt, Sapphire. You may marry him. You know that you and your sister's betrothal to Cowan and Jasper was called off when Topaz was sent away for her own protection. Now the Ocean Princess is coming home." He stood and announced the last bit to the whole audience, who came for the courting ceremonies to see which suitor I would choose. They liked to look at it as some kind of entertainment.

I looked over at Matt with a huge grin on my face. He saw the happiness in me and gave a weak smile, then swam away. I furrowed my eyebrows and shrugged. I rose and followed him as he disappeared into the servant's room. I called the head servant and asked for my hand-maiden, Ally, and Matt to both be excused of their duties.

I waited as both of them emerged from the kitchens. Ally came over and gave me a big hug and thanked me. I sent her to go and fetch the three of us something to eat, and motioned for Matt to follow me.

We swam up the staircase and into my room. It wasn't my chambers, but the room I liked to call my dining room. Most nights I ate alone with Grandfather in the room. I took my seat as Matt stood uncomfortably a few seats away, like he was scared he would get in trouble if he came to close.

I laughed. "You can sit down," I said.

He smiled, a real smile, and took a seat across from me.

"What's going to happen with you and Lord Shark? I don't think it worked out very well. Maybe the next suitor will be the one?" Matt said.

"I don't have anymore suitors who wish to marry me," I said.

"Every Prince and Lord wishes to marry you!" he said. "One of them must have liked you. Although you do put them on the spot when you go around raiding all of them."

"I find it amusing. They expect it be a man, not a girl. Let alone a Princess! Must all of them be so stupid?" I asked.

He smiled at me. There was something in his eyes, something that almost made him look normal. The absurdity that he could ever love me! I loved him, I knew that, but it was almost crazy to even think about it. He was a servant and I was a Princess. The legendary Land Princess! Making me out of his reach, and him out of mine.

I smiled and saw a glow in his eyes.

Ally walked through the door with a couple of other servants from the kitchen laden with food. The servants set the food on the table and then left the room. Ally grabbed herself a plate and piled food on top of it, then also left.

I laughed, "Ally hates dining with me. She claims that I am more polite when I am in court, then when people are interrupting me from eating my food."

Matt laughed. It was great to hear his laughs and it was always a blessing, because they didn't come that often. "I know you and you are a little temperamental when it comes to food."

"Hey!" I exclaimed as he laughed again.

I threw a roll at his head, which he caught in his hand and took a large bite out of it.

"What do you think's going to happen now that Topaz has entered the Ocean," I asked playing with the food on my plate.

"The war is close. It's the only way to get your dad back and you have to be involved Sapphire."

"If I go, will you come with me?" I asked.

Matt looked at me, like it was ludicrous to even suggest, because the question meant a lot more than how it was worded. He caught on to everything, especially this. He looked me right in the eyes. I felt like he was searching through me for something, something he could not find.

"Of course! Do you really think I would let you go into a war alone? You are my best friend. I won't abandon you, I can promise you that," Matt answered.

I smiled. Looking into my food, I was happy.

Tamina

We were soaring through the water, and I could think of a thousand words to describe the sunset. Beautiful, stunning, divine, enchanting, magnificent, exquisite, bewitching. I could go on forever.

The sun set and reflected against the slightly moving water, and spanning across the horizon were all different shades of pinks and purples, oranges and yellows. It was beautiful. I was intrigued until the sun finally vanished and the sky was engulfed in darkness, stars everywhere.

Everyone should be asleep, or getting there.

"You know, you do look a lot like your Father," a voice uttered from behind me. "The red-hair and grey eyes, everything else you have gotten from your Mother. I mean that as a compliment, Topaz. I loved your Mother and Father. They were my best friends. I helped your Mother sneak out to meet your Father a couple of times," he laughed.

I turned and saw Triton, standing there leaning casually on his sword which was digging into the already harsh wood of the deck.

"What are you doing out here? I have the watch tonight," I said.

"I thought you might need someone to practice with." He held up his sword, twirling it in his hand. "You know, I always practiced with your dad. He always thought that if he practiced at night he would be that much more aware in the daylight."

"Was he right?" I asked.

Triton laughed. "Yes."

I grabbed one of the swords from the rack. "Well, lets see how I do."

His white teeth glinted in the darkness.

The first blow came, but I was ready. Our swords crashed together. I leaned backwards on my left foot and put all of my weight into my swing. Triton blocked it, and pushed back towards me with his sword. I ducked and swept the deck with my foot, but he jumped. I stood back up and ran at him, my sword rose, and as he stuck his foot out I sidestepped just in time to avoid his foot to my gut. I twirled on the spot and faced him, the darkness clouding his face, but through the light of the moon I could see his silhouette. We parried, until I finally broke the contact, pushing him back a few steps.

My adrenaline was pumping. He ran at me, knocked the sword out of my hands, and then swung his sword at my legs. I launched into the air setting my hands on his shoulders and flipping myself over him. I landed on my feet and turned in just enough time to kick the sword out from my direction. I jumped into the air turning and sticking out my foot in a karate kick. My foot connected with something, and I fell towards the ground sideways. I stuck out my hands and when they touched the ground, I put all of my strength into pushing myself up and onto my feet again. I kicked the sword out of his hands, and began to see the crew up on deck gathering with their backs against the rails, watching us fight. Sky had a flashlight tinted pink following every move I made, and Jake held the other flashlight tinted blue, following Triton.

I laughed.

The sight distracted me. Triton's fist connected with my stomach and I flew backwards colliding into the wall. The jolt sent my senses up and running, my heart pounding. I got up and stepped away from the wall. I ran towards him, and jumped sideways, my feet angled at his face. If only he didn't push me away, I was flying towards the mast. I grabbed onto the mast. As I flew, the wood burned my hands. I propelled myself forward so that I moved around the mast without my feet touching the ground.

Triton turned at just the wrong moment and my feet knocked into his face. I let go of the mast and landed on the deck. My one knee just barely touched the ground and my fingers rested slightly on the wood just like I was about to race in a track event. I looked up and saw Triton stumbling to rise to his feet.

I casually stood and crossed my arms. He got up and looked at me, smiling. He raised his hands in surrender as the crew erupted into cheers.

I walked over to him and shook his hand. I was beaming.

"You really are his daughter aren't you?" Triton asked. "I couldn't have even done one of those moves."

I laughed, nodding my head. I had so many comebacks to throw right back at him, about him being older and slow. He was family and it seemed like something a niece would say to her uncle, but I wouldn't want to make the poor guy cry.

"Show's over, now everyone in bed. You should all be sleeping," I announced.

"I'll take the watch okay, Tam?" Thomas said.

"No, it's fine. I'm a big girl, I can handle it by

myself," I said smiling.

He smiled, turned and began to walk away. Guilt wrenched my stomach.

"Thomas, your welcome to stay out here though," I said quickly, before I could take back the words that escaped my mouth.

He turned around and laughed. "Okay-y."

The way he said the word made me laugh too. I looked up at the crows' nest, and remembered when we were little kids. Pamela would try to put me into dresses and play dress up and dolls. To escape, I would go outside and play with Thomas and Jack. We would have competitions, like climbing to the tops of the trees.

I waited until all the crew had gone below deck.

"Race you to the top," I said running over to the ropes.

"Ohh your so on," Thomas said chasing after me.

I gripped the ropes and hoisted my self higher and higher up. Then, my view started to blur and everything started to spin. I heard hissing, like the sound a snake makes when it's angry. I felt like even the softest wind could've knocked me off of the ropes. The voice was soft and consistent, and was circling all around me and wouldn't stop, leaving me to suffer the pain.

'I'm here. Topaz, I'm here. Don't worry. I'm on my way. It's Sapphire. I can hear you.'

The shock stabbed at my stomach, my heart was in my throat, and my hands went numb. I couldn't hold on any longer. My hands slipped, I lost my footing on the ropes and I fell backwards. I fell towards the water.

Jake

The scream rattled me from my sleep. Although, I wasn't really sleeping, but I was trying to. I had too much to think about, too much on my mind, too much to piece together to even try to figure out what was going on.

I jumped off of the hammock and started running. So did everyone else. It was almost a race, like the first one to the source of the scream, got Tamina's attention. I mean, she was amazing, she totally kicked Triton's butt, and came out of that fight without a scratch.

We all surfaced onto the deck, and as stupid as they were, Blake and Jayden were looking around the deck, swords in hands ready to kill. They needed some brains in those thick skulls of theirs.

I saw Thomas leaning over the railing, like he was looking for something. I quickly looked around and accounted for everyone. Everyone, except for Tamina.

I ran over to Thomas.

"What happened?" I asked

"I-I don't know. We were climbing to the crows' nest and then she was falling. I couldn't get over here in time." He stammered. "Jake, I think she's gone."

"Why didn't you jump?" I asked.

"I didn't even think about that." Thomas admitted and began to take off his shirt.

"What are you doing?" I exclaimed.

"I'm going to get her. She's the key to winning this war. We need both of the Princesses," he answered.

Thomas stepped onto the rail, and jumped. I looked over the railing and watched as he fell towards the water and landed with a splash. I waited and waited. It seemed to take forever for them to resurface, and when they did, Tamina was pulling Thomas up and I could see fins instead of legs treading the water to stay above the surface.

I yelled at Triton to grab a rope. I hopped from foot to foot waiting as I heard Tamina screaming at me. I finally took the rope from Triton and threw it over the edge, holding on to one of the ends. I felt the weight add onto the other end, and we started pulling them up.

We hauled them over the side of the rail and I grabbed Tamina's hand helping her up. Triton bent over, listening for Thomas' breath.

Tamina collapsed on the deck of the ship, coughing out water, and traces of blood, onto the deck. When she finished, she flopped onto her back and drew in a big breath as she lay shaking with her eyes squeezed shut. She dragged her hands up so they covered her face, and her shoulders began to shake. I walked over and sat down beside her shaking body.

"Hey, it's okay. It wasn't your fault," I said rubbing her shoulder.

"I fell off of the ropes. I had been trained not to do that when I sailed. I just, I couldn't - I didn't expect it to hurt so much. I couldn't hold on to it. My hands slipped, and all I remember is Thomas' face appearing below the water, and then his eyelids covered his eyes. He looked like he was suffocating, I had to do something," she gasped.

I furrowed my eyebrows. "What hurt?"

"I heard Sapphire. Jake, she's alive. She communicated to me, through the ocean. Just like I did to her.

She can hear me Jake. She's coming," Tamina said looking at me with her eyes shining with a certain glow in them. I furrowed my eyebrows at her, not understanding a word she said.

Tamina

I waited, clutching Thomas' hand until he woke up. He had been drifting in and out of consciousness for hours and it was beginning to scare me.

"Topaz, maybe you should give him some room. He might wake up if you weren't here breathing down his neck," Triton smirked.

I glared at him, stood and left the room. It was the first time I had been outside in a couple of hours, and the sun was so bright in the sky it began to make my head spin. Clutching the railing I steadied myself before I started to walk around again.

Bay walked over to me, a huge smile on her face. Blake, Jayden, and Mallory followed in her wake. "So you decided to emerge from the infirmary or whatever you're going to call that dungeon?" Bay asked.

I busted out laughing. It honestly was the first time, since the depths of the ocean almost killed Thomas that I had laughed. It made Bay's smile spread, becoming more of an ear-to-ear grin than a smile.

Then it hit me. A wave of nausea, and I stumbled forward, banging into Jayden as I almost fell over. Both Blake and Jayden were bent over trying to keep me on my feet. The hissing noise came back and I instantly saw an image. My sister, Sapphire, was covered in weapons and army gear. She was signaling to a boy to follow her. The boy was a stranger to my eyes. Although, he wasn't that bad to look at. He had these bright blue eyes, and jet-black hair that looked like it was constantly falling in his face. Sapphire looked over at the boy, her mouth curling into an admirable smile that reminded me so much of mine. What am I saying? Of course it would, we're identical twins!

I could tell that she admired him. Well, no not admired, more like loved him. You could tell by the way her storm gray eyes lit up just by looking at him. She seemed relaxed beside him.

The image blurred, like someone had thrown a rock into a still pond. It was rippled and made the vision, the only image I had of my sister, slip from my grasp.

I looked up to see everyone crowding around me, their faces inches from mine. I drew in a breath, and their faces blurred. I blinked a few times but then I slipped from the worlds grasp yet again and I watched as my vision disappeared.

I woke to someone laying a cool cloth on my forehead. I looked up blinking, and saw Thomas' face hovering over top of me. I breathed in his scent. The salt water of the ocean still lingered on his clothes.

I began to sit up, but was sent back into a spell of dizziness. Thomas placed a hand in the middle of my back and helped me sit up properly.

"What happened?" I asked rubbing my head, which was pounding.

"All I know is that I woke up when Blake and Jayden were laying you down on the bed. Honestly, they looked scared," Thomas said, looking at his hands.

"Thank you, for jumping in after me," I said.

"Didn't really help, did it?" Thomas said.

I shook my head. "You jumped in after me, you were trying to help me. That's what's really important. Thomas, at least you weren't walking around the ship with a sword in your hand looking for somebody to slaughter."

"Jake had to remind me to jump in after you," Thomas said setting his hands on his face.

"You still jumped in," I exclaimed.

He looked at me through his fingers. Running his hands through his hair, he exhaled. It was like he had been holding his breath for a long time and he finally was free enough to breathe.

I really did feel thankful that he at least jumped in after me.

I swung my legs over the side of the bed and stood up. I looked back at Thomas.

"I know you don't want to hear it Thomas, but sometimes, you need to hear that people care that you did something. You need to hear them say thank you." I exhaled, my voice not as steady as I would've wanted. "Thank you."

I walked out of the cabin, closing the door behind me. I leaned against it. Taking another deep breath, I walked to the rail.

I had never been seasick. From all the years of sailing, I had never had a cold, or a stuffed nose. I felt like I was going to be sick. I gripped the railing, looking into the ocean, which had started to darken. I felt like I was looking right into the heart of it, tapping into all of its secrets. I stared into my reflection's eyes. It wasn't moving like a normal reflection on water would. It started to rise towards me, up and out of the water.

I took a few steps back, tripping over my own feet and I fell to the ground.

I saw my identical twin set herself down on the railing. Her tail disappearing and turning into two legs.

"Hiyah sis!" Sapphire said grinning.

"Sapphire?" I asked.

She nodded, as a boy rose out of the water and onto the railing.

"Well, my day's officially been ruined. This is your evil twin Sapphire, Topaz. Don't worry your little heart though, you're still my favorite twin." Ryder said from behind me. His arms crossed over his chest, and his dark hair falling into his eyes.

"Oh shut up Ryder," Sapphire said jumping off of the rail and coming over to give me a big hug. I was honestly too shocked to return it.

"Topaz, wow you look so much like me!" Sapphire exclaimed.

"That's kind of the point of an 'identical twin' Saph," said the boy with her.

"Well, she does! Topaz, this is Matt," she said, with both enthusiasm and pride in her voice. Matt nodded at me.

"So, when is this war scheduled for? I have a very important guest visiting my place in 24 hours," Matt said jokingly.

"I don't know, honestly. We have been looking for the ship for the past two days. I haven't seen anything. Neither has anyone else."

"Oh, I know! Have you tried Dad's map yet?" Sapphire exclaimed.

I stared at her. I knew exactly what she was talking about. I just didn't want to admit that I hadn't thought of it.

She rolled her eyes at me. "You know the old looking piece of paper rolled up that Abigail gave to you only 48 hours ago? Yep, I definitely know who inherited the brains in this family."

Ryder set his hand on my shoulder. "Hey Topaz, it's okay, she just thinks she has the brains. We all know that I do."

He twirled his hands around a little bit and ended up pointing at himself. He had a stuck up grin on his face that made me snort with laughter.

"Sure Ryder, whatever gets you through the day," Sapphire said coming up beside him and patting his shoulder.

I laughed again and covered my mouth with my hand.

"Tamina, who are you talking to now?" Thomas said joining us.

I waited, and watched as his eyes flew from me then to Sapphire, then back to me. He knelt on one knee, his head bent over. "My apologies, your Majesty. I didn't know you had embarked the ship."

"Get up Thomas, you're embarrassing us," I said looking around at the rest of the crew.

Thomas scrambled to his feet and I could hear Matt snickering in the background. Thomas glared at him.

"What you laughing at?" Thomas said, his face turning to stone.

What's his problem? I thought to myself.

"Just the fact that Topaz has got you wrapped around her little finger." Matt smirked pointing to me. "You obviously don't know of the courting rituals for the Ocean Princess. Yet, you are familiar with the stance when in the presence of a royal. She couldn't have taught you that."

My body tensed and I saw that Thomas' hands had curled into fists at his sides.

"Matt don't," Sapphire started.

"Sapphire, don't you understand? Thomas gets to talk to Topaz without getting whipped or being threatened to loose his job. I've had to go through that since I met you, it's not fair. We couldn't be together, but they can." Matt interrupted.

Sapphire sighed and looked at her feet.

"We could be together now, Matt." Sapphire whispered to Matt.

Sapphire gave me a look, sending me a silent plea of help through her eyes.

"Thomas and I are not together Matt. You have to be stupid to think that we were," I said, instantly wishing I could take back the words.

I could see Thomas' jaw set and lock in place as he turned and left our little gathering. I began to open my mouth to say something, but he turned to look at me just as I opened it, sending a shiver up my spine. If looks could kill, I would be dead three times over. Through his death stare I could see the look of disappointment, and sadness in his eyes. I felt like melting into the background, like jumping ship, just so that I wouldn't have to look into his eyes. His gaze held, and I was forced to look away.

Jake

I watched Thomas storm away from the group that seemed to be floating out of the ocean. The look on his face was definitely from hurt and maybe even a little guilt.

I shook off the itch to walk over to Tamina and slap her. Instead, I was knocked off my feet by a substantial force to the ship. The ship lurched forward and I could see Bay and Mallory straining to keep ahold of one of the ropes. With a hard and painful effort, the rope slipped from their grasp and one of the large oak masts started swinging. I slowly got to my feet and everything seemed to be spinning.

All of a sudden huge green monsters rose from the sides of the ship and climbed aboard. All produced large scythe like weapons, except for the long knives protruding out of the opposite end.

I gripped the knife handle in my pocket, and took it out as one of the monstrous creatures made their way towards me. He swung at my legs. I jumped and sliced my blade towards him, but he sidestepped it. I landed on my feet as he poked the knife end at me, and using my knife I deflected it. I kicked him in the gut and my knife slipped from my grasp. It went flying through the air and dug deep into the creatures' chest as it fell to the ground lifeless. I quickly bent over the Thing and wrenched the knife out of him.

"Jake!" A voice screamed.

I turned around and found Tamina facing me. She

tossed me an extra sword and then quickly turned around and began fighting again. Tamina was moving with such grace and agility that it was almost a dance.

I heard a grunt from behind me, and I turned just in time to see a beast leaning over me with it's staff raised above it's head ready to come down on me. I sidestepped out of the way and I heard a thunk as the knife dug into the wood. I stepped heavily onto its blade and brought the sword down on it. The wood snapped in half and the beast went stumbling backwards. I spun around and the sword went smack dab right through his heart.

I felt someone's body press against my back and turned my head slightly. I got a face full of brown hair and recognized Bay's height and stance. I relaxed a little.

It sort of turned into a dance between her and I. We both fought, backs pressed against each other's, except for the occasional trouble swing, where we'd switch spots and fight the others opponent. They all went down in the end.

I was exhausted, but I still stood and anticipated another one of those demon creatures to step up and challenge us. They slowly retreated and we both collapsed beside each other.

I watched closely as Tamina fought. Her face was contorted with concentration as she continued to shrug off her opponent's strikes. I laughed. She looked away from her partner and smiled and then the hooked part of the staff came down on her arm. I watched it break into her skin as she crumpled a little. I started to get to my feet, but I stopped. She swiped her blade to the under arm of the beast and it screamed. Swinging the knife part of its staff towards her, it caught her forehead and she went down to the ground. Her sword clattering away from her, I watched it slide through a hole in the rail and topple over into the ocean. Unfortunately, the beast was winning, though not for long. Tamina launched herself into the air and swept her foot across the floor, knocking the giant thing to the ground. She stepped back and observed as everyone dog-piled on top of the monster and Matt brought the knife down on its heart.

Tamina screamed.

Everyone looked up at her in surprise and quickly climbed off of the thing. Tamina went down on her knees. I could see why, as the thing didn't look much older than us. It was a girl and it was ugly. It's skin peeled away from its face and it was a sickly green, almost like it was going to throw up.

It also started to look a lot like Pamela Parker.

Tamina

I collapsed onto the ground next to the mast and pulled my knees up to my chest. All that was running through my head was; that was Pamela that was Pamela! What the heck was going on?

I felt like I had been kicked in the stomach. I knew it couldn't have been her. I could feel someone pull me away from the dead body and looked up to find Jake. I hadn't seen Jake in such a while that I had forgotten he was on the ship.

I let him help me up and I lost my balance on the deck. Sort of staggering towards the rail, I looked over.

There, looking up at me, were more of those creatures. There were hundreds of them sitting just below the water. I felt nauseous. If all of those things jumped onto the ship and started attacking us, we wouldn't even stand a chance.

My vision blurred for a second. It went a little red, and I could smell the metallic scent of blood. My hand went to my forehead and it stung. I pulled my hand back quickly to find that it was coated in blood. The sight of my own blood almost sent me spinning again but I kept my eyes focused and concentrated. I couldn't freak out now. I gripped the railing and could see the little bits of wood scraping off from my outgrown nails. I exhaled the breath I had been holding and began to breathe normally. I closed my eyes and breathed in the salty ocean spray, which burned the inside of my nose.

I remembered when I was a little kid, and every night I would sneak out and go to the beach. There, I would sit on the rocks and think out scenarios, the scenarios of how these classes would come to any use. All of them involved Aunt Bea getting kidnapped and me trying to prove myself to her. Proving that I wasn't a waste of space, like she referred to my Father as. I wanted to be different than him. I didn't want to abandon people as he had abandoned me, forcing me to think I was all alone.

I still don't. I opened my eyes. It was beginning to get dark out and I watched as everyone cleaned up and started heading, one by one, off to bed. Soon I was the only one left.

I shook my head. Looking up I saw, in the place of the northern star, a green one, blinking at me. I squinted my eyes. It wasn't a passing airplane. Not a rocket. It had to be a star.

I set the light to the back of my head. These little problems are not going to help me get my Father back.

I heard somebody step onto the deck. I turned around, and was shot in the eyes with salt water. If you have ever gotten salt water in the eye, you would know that it hurts like hell! Then, I saw a shadow. A silhouette in the light that walked towards me. It posed little threat, but I still gripped the knife stuck in my belt. It was inches away from me and I had to tilt my head up. It was a boy, with shining blue eyes and short brown hair. He looked at me. He was taller than me by a couple inches and was really handsome.

"Topaz? Is that you?" he asked.

I narrowed my eyes. "Yeah. Who are you?" I

asked.

"You don't know my name?" he asked, taking a couple steps back. He almost looked hurt. "Don't you remember me?"

I shook my head. Taking two steps forward we were toe to toe again.

"No, I don't. Could you tell me?" I asked.

He looked around almost frantically, as if he were calling out for help. Then he sighed. "We were betrothed by your Grandfather at birth. When you disappeared, it was broken. My sister is going to marry your brother Ryder. You really don't know who I am?" he asked.

My heart sank for this boy. "No ... Wait. Maybe I do."

A bang came from somewhere in the distance. I don't know what it was or where it came from but it spooked the boy. I kept my ears pricked, but didn't turn my head. I just kept looking at the boy.

"What's your name?" I asked.

"Jasper," he whispered, only loud enough that I could hear.

I smiled. "Great to meet you, Jasper."

He grabbed my hands with his and they were really cold. "You're beautiful you know that Topaz? I'd heard how the Princesses were more beautiful than all the mermaids in the ocean but, I didn't believe it until now."

"Thank you," I said, my cheeks growing hot. "Your hands are really cold."

His eyes shone. Stars reflected off of them making them shine even more. "Can you tell where I'm from just by how cold my hands are?"

"No." I answered.

"I am from the deepest part of the ocean. My

people don't usually come out in the light. We are used to the darkness of the ocean floor, but I had to see you."

With those words my heart officially melted. He leaned over and kissed me. His lips were soft. He pulled away and we both looked at each other. I leaned over to him, put my hands on his shoulders and kissed him again. My cheeks grew hotter. My first kiss. Definitely one of the highlights of this rescue mission. He kissed me back putting his hands on my waist and pulling me closer. This time I pulled away. I smiled and hugged him, as he hugged me back. His arms were solid around me. We both let go of each other. He grabbed my hand, bowed and kissed it.

He whispered in my ear. "Good-bye."

"Bye." I whispered back.

I was almost frozen right there on the spot. It was a scary feeling. I had never felt that vulnerable. Jasper walked over to the edge of the railing, climbed on top and jumped off. I held back a scream as I ran over to the railing. There was no splash. He floated up to me.

"You can fly?" I asked taken aback.

"No, I'm standing on water," he answered laughing.

I smiled again. His laugh was carefree and I liked it. He placed a hand on my cheek, a cold hand.

"Will I ever see you again?" I asked.

"I don't know," Jasper answered, taking his hand away and sank further into the water. His head was just above the water as he said, "I hope so."

Then he disappeared into the dark ocean.

Jasper

I sank into the ocean, not losing eye contact with her. I found her, I found Topaz! I can't believe it. I can't wait to tell Jordan, Cowan and Dad. I went zipping through the ocean, through the doors of the castle and into the throne room.

"Father! Father, I found her!" I panted.

"What?" My father said standing. Jordan sat across her throne with her tail over one end and her head hanging over the other. She was checking her nails and her tiara was hanging on the edge of her throne. Jordan looked over at me. Rolling her eyes, she swiped her black hair out of her chestnut brown eyes and sat up.

Jordan was my older half-sister. Her mother was a human; mine was the Queen at the moment. At a young age, Jordan was sent to Victoria to keep watch over Topaz and to ensure her whereabouts. On land, Jordan was known as Pamela Parker and lived the life of a human.

Jordan set the tiara on top of her head and swept her hair up, pinning it back in a ponytail with a few strands falling out.

We glared at each other.

"I found Princess Topaz, Father!" I repeated myself.

Jordan's face went pale. "Don't be absurd! I led the Night Devils right to her little hideout. She is dead. No one could outrun, or out hunt them and live to tell the tale."

"Well, she's alive Jordan! Looks like little miss perfect missed a little itsy, bitsy detail on that hunt."

"What is that brother?" she asked harshly.

"Topaz was trained like a Night Devil. She is just as fast and she can outrun them, and she's hunting us down because of him!" I said, losing my temper and pointing to the cage hanging above us. The cage that was holding Matthew Jackson, the Father of Topaz, Sapphire and Ryder. Despicable!

"Topaz doesn't care about her Father. She is just looking to find out who she really is genius. If she did find this mongrel she'd help us slaughter him for abandoning her in her time of need. You got that?"

"Children, children. We have hit an unfortunate bump in the road to gain power of all parts of the ocean. All we have to do is kill the Land and Ocean Princesses and make sure that Ryder inherits every bit of land that they own. Then, once Ryder and Jordan marry, all will be left to her in the unfortunate event that he dies," my Father jumped in as usual.

"Jordan has already failed to kill Topaz and Sapphire. How exactly are we supposed to kill either of them when they are slipping from our grasp? We need to stop them before they get any stronger," I said quickly.

Jordan glared at me and then quickly looked back to our Father, than back to me and than to our Father once again.

"Obviously you don't understand me when I say that I will handle this, and I can handle this! So, stop investigating and work on getting what needs to be done, done. You planned the party for my engagement tomorrow, yes?" Jordan asked.

I moaned. My temper grew as I spoke through gritted teeth, "yes, sister."

"When tomorrow? I need to look fantastic in the Upland's light," Jordan questioned.

I rolled my eyes at her. "Noon, when the sun is at its peak."

Jordan grinned.

"Now enough talk about engagements," Dad said again. "What did Topaz look like?"

I laughed. "She's beautiful. Her eyes, even in the moonlight, look like the ocean in one of its fits. Her hair is a fiery red and she's even prettier than Jordan." I stuck that last comment in just for the pure joy of Jordan's reaction. It was true though.

"How dare you?" she screeched. "I am more beautiful than her and everyone knows it! She is just a little prissy girl who can hold a sword. Every boy falls in love with her because she can cut their heart out, feed it to the dogs and not even care. She has never loved anyone but herself." Jordan swam as quickly as she could out of the room.

I grinned as my Mother came swimming into the room. My Mom was a Lowland creature, one that could change shape. That's why she looked like a mermaid now, and that's how I can grow legs when on land.

"What did you do to Jordan now, Jasper? Her engagement is tomorrow, you should be keeping her calm, not setting fire to her temper," Mother laughed and scolded at the same time.

"I did absolutely nothing but say that the Ocean Princess is far more beautiful than her, which is true," I defended myself.

"You found her? Well, won't Poseidon be pleased to hear that his Granddaughter has been found. Oh, and poor Sapphire shall be pleased as well, her twin coming home. Perhaps she will be at Jordan and Ryders' wedding. That'll make two bridesmaids other then Jasmine. Oh no! More planning," Mom began mumbling to herself and swam quickly out of the room.

I looked at my Father who I could tell was waiting for my Mother to be out of the room.

"You think she is beautiful?" My Father asked.

I nodded.

"Then it is your job to kill her," he said and swam out of the room.

I looked at my brother Cowan, my fraternal twin. He hadn't spoken through the entire conversation. "You can't do it, Jasper. You know how hard we've worked to get this far. We were betrothed to those two girls, they'll know it was us and we won't be able to live with the hatred. I've met Sapphire, spoken to her in person. Neither of them did anything. Sapphire just wanted her sister back."

I nodded. "If I don't do this, whose going to help us brother?" I asked.

Jake

Nothing was going the way we expected. We had no idea where we were going, were almost out of food, and Tamina was off in her own little world. At least that was how it seemed for a while.

Everyone started to tense up. They were whispering together and Bay and I started to freak out. I was now having constant visions. They were always of the same thing. Tamina falling into the water, blood soaking through her shirt. She was always wearing this white blouse and then as she was sinking into the ocean, a brown haired boy stood by sobbing as he watched Tamina fall. But the boy wasn't Thomas. I thought that it should be Thomas. Why wasn't it Thomas?

I had told Bay what I was seeing. She was the only one so far that knew. She turned around to me, "I still think you should tell Tamina about what you're seeing. It could help. I swear we've seen that bunch of coral a million times. I think we're going in circles. Maybe telling her would help," Bay said.

"Yeah, I wonder how that conversation would work out. 'Hey Tamina, yeah, I just thought I should let you know that I've been seeing things and you and your sister are gonna die. Oh, and did I mention that you have this stalker kid crying over your dead body?" I rolled my eyes.

"Hey, don't get all crabby with me, I'm just trying to help!" Bay snapped back. "You know, you might think that you're the only one who's lost something or someone that they've loved, but you have no idea what I've been through."

She got up and started walking away. "Wait, Bay. I'm sorry, I can be a jerk sometimes."

"Yeah. I agree with that Jake, but you really should think about talking to Tamina, about what's going on with your head. You might need some serious help."

I gasped at her as she walked away. Help? She's not serious right? There is nothing wrong with me. Right?

Tamina

"Tamina, can we talk to you for a second?" A knock came from the door.

I looked up from the map and the desk of the Captain's quarters. "Yeah, come on in."

The door opened and Thomas and Jack walked in. Thomas looked absolutely furious. They shut the door. Jack leaned against it, his arms folded across his chest. Thomas walked around the desk, got down on his knees, took my face in his hands and kissed me.

My eyes widened at the sudden change in composure in Thomas. I instantly pushed him away.

"What the heck are you doing?" I asked, trying to keep my voice steady. I still remembered the kiss with Jasper. You can't really forget your first kiss, has anyone ever tried? Does anyone ever really want to?

"I knew it. You don't like me anymore do you?" Thomas asked.

I looked at him, right in his eyes. I could see it again, the sadness. I liked him once, but that didn't last long. Now he's just kissing me. Too little, too late bud. I stood up.

"Who said I ever did?" I said.

He glared at me and I raised my eyebrows, daring him to do anything. He stepped away from me.

"But ... but you ... you never ... am I just another

one of your friends? Do you really think you can just play with my feelings?" Thomas asked.

"No! Why would you even think that I liked you as anything more than a friend? How would you have ever even thought that?" I snapped.

"You always talked to me, smiled at me, you never agreed with anybody but me ..." he said his voice drifting away.

"You thought that just because I consider you a close friend, and I value your opinion, that it means that I like you as more than a friend? Are you really that conceited?" I asked.

"Well, I'm sorry Tamina if I don't go around tricking people, getting people to think highly of you, while I have to sit back and watch you kiss other boys," he snapped back, talking quickly and quietly.

I took in a sharp intake of air, and my stomach felt as if I had just been punched in the stomach. He saw me kiss Jasper! That's what this was all about.

"Is that what this is about? You think that because you weren't my first kiss, it means that you can come and poke your nose in my business. Thomas, I thought I could trust you more!"

"That's exactly what I was going to say to you Tamina. You don't even know this guy. You just figure that because he knows you, you can go and kiss him. What happened to the Tamina that I used to know?"

"She grew up. She doesn't care about what people look like. Just because you think you're so perfect, that every single girl would fall in love with you in a matter of seconds, doesn't mean I can't be the first one to say no," I snapped back.

Standing, I put both of my hands on his chest and shoved him backwards. "I don't want to be the one to say yes to you, I don't like being controlled. You should know that Thomas."

He stumbled backwards knocking into the wall. Jack moved starting to come between us.

I put up my hand. "Don't you dare Jack!"

He spread his hands and stepped back to the door. Thomas looked at me, finally showing some fear. He was scared of me and I relished that thought. Thomas, the friend I've had since I went to live with Aunt Bea, the boy who never backed away, never lost a fight, who always shrugged off suspensions, who always wanted to protect me, was scared of a tiny 5 foot 2 inched tall, redheaded girl.

"I am not going to be your girl. I never was. I never will be, Thomas. Get that through your thick skull! I don't want you to be able to put me in a trophy room, Thomas. You don't know what I have to deal with. I don't ever want to be the prized collector item of any boy. EVER! Especially not you," I said going to sit back down.

I saw his fist come but I didn't try to react. I took it like I was made of steel. Until it actually connected. Thomas threw a punch at my face! His knuckles connected solidly with my forehead. I stumbled backwards and landed in my chair. Tears sprung to my eyes and I set my head in my hands. I broke down, and for the first time in what felt like years, I cried.

I quickly regained my composure and stood up. I glared at him. I felt my left eye protesting and it stung. His face was red with anger, but he showed the surprise of his actions in his expression.

I sat, trying to control my breathing and hold back the rest of my tears, which I did manage to control. The back of my eyes burned and itched. My bottom lip quivered so much I had to bite it so that it would stop.

"See, this is why I could never like you more than I do as a friend! You can't control your anger and you can't control your actions. You will never be able to win me over." That was all it took.

Another fist came, this time connecting with my jaw. I bit deeper into my lip. I could feel the blood running down my chin, and could taste it in my mouth as my teeth dug into the inside of my cheek.

"Tamina, are you okay?" Jack asked rushing over to me. Putting a hand to the bruise forming above my eye.

I held back a sob and nodded my head. "Can you guys just leave now?"

"Yeah, I'm so sorry Thomas did that Tam. I didn't think that he would do that. He just said he needed to talk to you and that he wanted me to come with him."

I sort of smiled at him. At least I hope it was a smile. "I-I'm fine. Can you guys leave now?"

"Tamina, I'm so sorry," Thomas said, fighting against Jack. "Please, forgive me Tamina. I didn't mean it."

"Thomas, just leave. Do me a favor ... don't talk to me," I said.

Thomas looked at me, his eyebrows raised at an angle. He stopped fighting Jack, who successfully forced him through the door. Jack closed it behind him.

I bent over the desk. Sobbing, some of my blood

dripped onto the map. I sniffed, and quickly used the sleeve of my sweater to try and wipe it away. It stayed in a perfect little dot and melted into the blank canvas. The canvas I had just spent seven hours trying to decipher and wondering why it wasn't showing me the way. The answer finally appeared with a tiny drop of my blood. All of a sudden, these little dots of land started appearing, drawing themselves onto the page. I swallowed a mouthful of blood. Then it started to draw our ship, then a castle popped up. Underneath of it, it said that there was an army of creatures coming, and how many days we had until they got to our location. We had less than two days.

Another knock at the door. "Tamina, it's Jake. Can I talk to you please? It's important."

"Umm, how important?" I asked.

"Well, I have been having these visions and there isn't going to be a happy ending." He answered, hesitating a little.

"Come in," I said.

He opened the door and when he saw my face, his own lit up with concern. "What the heck happened to you?" Jake asked.

"Thomas got mad at me," I answered.

"So he hit you!" he exclaimed giving me an instant feeling of relief.

"Yes, but that's not the point Jake. You wanted to talk to me about something involving the ship. Something about you seeing the future, not a good turnout?" I asked, quickly changing the subject.

"Oh yeah. I've been having these visions. These pictures running through my head. They all involve you falling into the ocean and drowning after being stabbed in the chest by ... by Pamela. There is a kid our age, crying over your dead body as we reel it up from the ocean," he said twiddling his thumbs and looking at his hands. He almost looked like he was thumb-wrestling himself.

I looked at him. "You're serious?"

He nodded his head.

"Thanks Jake, I've got to get back to navigating. Please, if the visions change come and tell me," I said bending my head back over the map.

"Okay, well, thanks for listening." He turned and walked out the door, shutting it quietly behind him.

This is it, I thought to myself. We finally had a war on our hands. I was going to win this, fighting to rescue my Father, for my Kingdom, or die trying. Guess my future had already been decided for me.

Jake

Seeing Tamina vulnerable made me sick. The thought that Thomas hit her was disgusting and made me mad. I shut the door quietly behind me.

Bay rushed up to me and engulfed me in her arms. I felt safe, although I couldn't help feeling a little weak at the same time, having a girl there to comfort me. I hugged her back. She backed up a couple steps, letting go of me.

"Did you tell her?" she questioned looking up at me, as I was almost half a foot taller.

"Yeah, and now I have something to say to Thomas," I said looking around.

"Why? What happened?" she pressed on.

"Thomas hit her, Bay. He got mad and smacked or punched or did something to make her mouth bleed. She looks bad, Bay," I said shaking my head, my eyes still scanning the deck.

There he was. Thomas was laughing with Jack, Blake, and Jayden. I jumped down the stairs, going two at a time and strode over to Thomas. I guess my fury showed on my face. I could hear Bay calling my name, but I pushed her voice to the back of my head.

"What's up Jake?" Thomas asked sliding his hands into his pockets.

I punched him in the stomach. He went reeling forward, his hands flying to his gut and I could hear his breath leave him as he gasped for air.

Nobody came to his defense. "What in the world

gives you the right to hit a girl? Huh?"

"I-I-I ... I swear I didn't mean to. If I could take back what I did, I would," he stammered through breaths.

"That still isn't a reason," I said my voice getting stronger.

"Why are you defending her anyway Jake? She's using us Jake. She doesn't care."

"She's my best friend. Thomas you cared about her. You couldn't get her out of your mind. You even admitted that to me, you admitted that to everyone. You have no right to change your mind and decide that she needs to be hurt." This time I yelled.

Thomas stumbled backwards and I looked past him at an older person rising out of the water.

"Grandpa!" Sapphire shouted, calling out to him.

He got closer to us, but he just looked blankly at her. Like he didn't recognize her. Like he had no idea who she was. Tamina was, in a matter of seconds, right beside Sapphire shouting, and screaming along with her sister. Again the old man just looked at them blankly, like he had forgotten who they were.

"Who are you?" he finally shouted back.

"I'm Sapphire. Grandpa don't you remember?" Sapphire shouted out.

Tamina immediately stopped and stepped back a couple of feet. The ocean began to rage, absolutely scream. Rocking the boat back and forth, the waves crashed against the side of the boat, as the old man drifted down into the ocean.

The waves were tsunami huge and got larger and larger, beginning to crash down onto the deck. Tamina, Sapphire and Ryder, all had their hands up and their faces contorted with concentration. They seemed to catch the biggest wave just before it hit us. We were literally lying on the ground when the wave stopped inches before our faces. The wave started to retreat, and slowly back away from us. I watched and spotted a couple of fish that had gotten caught in the wave, just swimming like they were in tsunami waves on a regular basis.

"Jake!" Bay screamed. I sat up and she came rushing over to me.

She helped me up, and shoved a knife into my hand. I put the knife in my belt. I stared at her, right into her hazel eyes, grabbed her face in my two hands and kissed her. She kissed me back. We broke apart when people started screaming again. I looked at her and we both grinned.

Jordan

The crown was woven seaweed. Not real seaweed, but golden threads woven together to look like it. I placed it on my head. Wow, I looked gorgeous.

My Father came bursting through the door to my room. "Is the King dead or not?" he asked.

I narrowed my eyes at him. "Yes, why wouldn't he be? You can control the water better than you could before now. No?" I asked.

"Yes, but I was not able to crush the boat, or snap it in half. I can hear all the little humans scream in terror." He pressed the tips of his fingers together and smiled maliciously.

"Okay, dad you're kinda creeping me out. Did you ever stop to think that there are four mermaids on that ship with the powers to control the ocean too? With the Land and Ocean Princesses together now they are stronger than you will ever be," I said, turning back to the floor length mirror. I fluffed my hair a little and then turned back to him. He glared at me. I even thought I could see little flames flickering in his eyes, but that was just a trick of the light. He raised the staff and pointed it at me. The small oval-shaped sapphire gem, and little topaz began to light up. I watched the water circle in around me, around my throat. It tightened. Tightened so much my vision began to blur just as he released me. I gasped for air, dropping to the ground. I was panting.

"How about you try it Jordan?" he shoved the staff in my face.

I grabbed it carefully and swam out of the room. Down the hall servants applauded me and shrunk back into the walls. I must have looked furious, and strikingly beautiful. I burst open the door to the throne room and in front of me was a huge screen revealing the storm happening above us. The waves were crashing constantly into the boat. It was on the verge of tipping over on a 45-degree angle, and then it was up again, straight and rocking with the waves.

I raised the staff to the screen. I closed my eyes, feeling the tension in the room. I was whispering the words King Poseidon whispered to me in his sickness. I envisioned the boat cracking down the middle, snapping, and the crew sinking down into the ocean for all the carnivorous creatures to eat. I opened my eyes. The boat was still whole and the waves had subsided. I narrowed my eyes and clenched my jaw. Then I lost it. I threw the staff to the ground and screamed at the top of my lungs.

"THE STUPID THING WON'T WORK! AHHH!" I yelled.

My brothers came up to me and grabbed my arms. My crown went tumbling off of my head.

"Calm down Jordan. It's just a ship. Calm down!" Cowan whispered to me.

I took a couple of deep breaths and stormed out of the room. I ripped open the doors to my wardrobe. My eyes landed on my black Night Devil outfit. The outfit I wore on expeditions with the Devils. I pulled it out and flung it onto my bed. I took out the long knife hidden in the piles of clothing. I stared at my reflection in the knife and pursing my lips, I smiled.

No, let me rephrase that. I grinned at the thought of finally getting rid of the only other girls in the world that were prettier than I was. I've tried every other way. That didn't work. Now it was personal.

Part 2

The Battle

Tamina

The wave subsided a little. It seemed to be collecting a breath and then came back twice as hard. The force of the wave was so strong I fell to my knees. With all of my strength, I focused my mind on the water and it lifting me off of my knees and back onto my feet as the wave folded upwards. Ryder gave a frustrated scream and the wave dissipated. I collapsed to my knees again. Breathing deeply, I saw stars from the strain of keeping us above water.

I got to my feet and went over to Sapphire to see if she was okay. I quickly shook her and she looked faintly at me as her eyes rolled into her head and she fell unconscious.

"Matt!" I shouted.

He came rushing over to Sapphire's side.

"I've never dealt with an unconscious person. Can you help me with this?" I asked.

He nodded his head numbly. "She'll be okay right?" he asked, looking over at me with dread and concern flowing through his eyes and face.

I nodded my head. "Yeah, of course she will," I answered. I looked back down at my sister. She looked almost peaceful and that made me smile.

"Topaz," a voice whispered over to me. It was more of a hiss over the ocean. It increased in volume and the voice began to sound like nails on a chalkboard. I pressed my hands over my ears, hoping to block out the noise. "Topaz, I know you're there. You can't hide from me anymore. We've killed your family. Your Aunt, and your Mother are dead. Your Grandfather and your Father are slowly dying."

I held back a scream and looked around. Everyone was staring at me. I felt the horror seep through my head and into my face. I felt tears burning at the back of my eyes as I held them back.

"What do you want from me?" I screamed.

The voice boomed with laughter, screeching at a high note that could make your ears bleed. "I want you dead."

Then, the voice faded away. The ocean returned to normal and I looked at Ryder. "What are we going to do now?" he asked me.

I shook my head. "Hide for now? I don't know. I think that island would be a good place."

"We can't hide. They can find us. They're killing Grandpa and taking away his immortality. They can find us now. Topaz, I think we should just wait it out. Let them find us, then surprise them by being ready for them," Ryder said crossing his arms.

"You can wait this out Ryder, but I want to see my Dad. I'm going to go save him. Don't try to stop me Ryder. I'll be back in an hour and if I'm not, tell everyone I will miss them, okay?" I stepped over, kissed him on the cheek and gave him a huge hug. He practically strangled me in return. I gripped the handle of the sword in my belt. I walked over to the rail and slipped out of my sneakers, socks, and jacket. I stepped barefoot onto the railing and I dove off crashing into the water. I opened my eyes and there was that feeling again. The feeling like I was the water. Scales began to form on my legs as they melted together, forming a tail. My   shirt melted away into the water, and my hair broke through my ponytail, making it feel the cleanest it had in days. A bikini type top covered my chest and I felt lightweight, like aluminum foil, making me feel really vulnerable. I started swimming to the bottom of the ocean.

Jake

I grabbed Bay's hand and hid with her in the weapons room underneath of a table piled with knives and pistols. I grabbed two of each, stuffing them in between my belt and my shorts. Bay looked at me, terror shining in her eyes. I wrapped my arm around her. Pulling her close, I put my chin on top of her head, breathing in the vanilla scent of her hair.

Bay's breathing became ragged and scared as thumps came from outside. The swords started shaking, and some began falling onto the table and floor. I put my hand over her mouth lightly as the knives and swords that had lain on racks on the walls began to shake off and stick themselves into the table.

The door crept open. I pulled my legs up to my chest so that we were hopefully out of sight of whoever had entered.

Bay's breathing calmed down a bit. I slowly pulled my hand away from her mouth, wrapped my other arm around her and kissed the top of her head. I prayed to God that she couldn't hear my heart pounding in my chest.

"Jake? Bay?" the voice hissed. "Are you in here?"

I held back the urge to speak.

"It's me Mallory. Please tell me you two are in here. Those green monsters have started attacking again and I need a place to hide."

I pulled Bay out from beneath the table along with me.

"Oh, thank God I found you!" Mallory exclaimed, but it wasn't Mallory who I was staring at. It was her double in Night Devil form.

It smiled at us with its' yellowed teeth poking out. Bay screamed from beside me, picked up a knife and chucked it at its chest.

Mallorys' look-a-like fell down right into me, dead. I shoved it off of me.

I looked to Bay and said, "we have to go help the others."

"Jake, but what if we get killed? I don't want to die. I just wanted some adventure this summer. I didn't think this was going to happen."

I turned to her and grabbed her shoulders. "Hey, look at me."

Bay tilted her head up slightly, tears shining in her eyes.

I leaned in, kissed her softly on the lips, and pulled away a tiny bit so that my lips were still brushing up against hers as I whispered, "I don't care if we don't survive. I've finally found someone that understands me. I won't ever leave your side, even if I die in this war."

Bay had her eyes closed, but she slowly nodded her head.

I kissed her again and this time she kissed me back. Bay pulled away, and took in a deep breath. "You ready to fight?" she asked.

"As long as I'm with you, I'm ready."

Bay stood up and grabbed my hand, quickly pulling me up. I stepped forward, grabbing one of the only swords still hanging on a rack. I gripped the doorknob so hard my knuckles went white and I looked back at Bay. She had a handful of knives in each hand. She nodded her head.

I slowly opened it. Cracking the door slightly open so that we could both fit through, without opening it all the way. The light of the moon shone down on us just enough that if you squinted you could probably see our faces.

I heard screaming. I pulled Bay down behind one of the gunpowder barrels.

"No! Don't you dare touch her Cowan. You've betrayed your family name! You've betrayed her!" Matt was screaming at someone.

I tilted my head up slightly so I could see what was going on.

A boy with fair hair, was holding Sapphire's arm tightly enough that you could see bruises forming from where I was.

"I won't hurt her, I promise Matt. I came here to protect her. I wouldn't do anything that stupid. She's the Land Princess, and she can help me and Jasper fix what we've done," Cowan countered.

"I love how no one's asking me what I want to do, and that you are talking about me and I'm right here!" Sapphire snapped at the two of them, struggling against Cowan's iron grip on her arm.

"Sapphire. I know you won't believe me, but your sister is down in our territory trying to get your Dad back. Ryder is fighting for his life, hoping to distract people so that Topaz will be able to get into The Underland Palace. My brother, Jasper, still thinks that killing the Jacksons' is the right thing to do, but I know it's not. Please forgive me, and trust me when I say that they need your help. You and your sister, Topaz, together will be stronger even than my Father," Cowan begged. "Please help them."

Sapphire looked at Cowan right in the eyes, stopped struggling, and then looked at Matt. I could see Night

Devils crawling over the rail, and making their way toward them. I stood up and shouted, "look out!"

Sapphire shook off Cowan, and the weapon of the tallest Devil sank into his heart. The knife went right through his chest, leaving three inches of the knife sticking out of his back. I closed my mouth to hold back the bile. Bay pulled me back down behind the barrel. Letting go of my arm, she got up and ran across the deck towards the Devils.

"No!" I shouted at her, but she ignored my shout.

Bay jumped at one of the creatures, sticking her knife into its back and holding on. Another tried to stab her as she clung on. She dropped to the floor as the staff went into the other Night Devil's back. The staff was pulled out, and Bay was stabbed at again. She barrel rolled to the side, throwing a knife right into the creature's chest. It came crashing down as she rolled off to the side again, just in time to avoid being squashed. She pushed off the deck and onto her feet again. Bay kicked up at its face and it stumbled backwards. She threw a punch at its gut, and the Night Devil went falling into the water. Another Night Devil grabbed ahold of her neck, lifting her off the ground. Bay dropped the knives in her hands and struggled against the Devil's grip.

I stood up, aimed the gun in my hand at its head, and I pulled the trigger.

Tamina

"What are you doing here?" I hissed at Ryder as I pressed my back against a wall of the castle.

"I'm going to help," he hissed back. "Oh, I forgot to wish you happy birthday sis!"

"What?" I asked. "It's not my birthday."

"Yes, it is. You and Saph were born on July 1, numero uno. That's today."

"No, I was born on November 18. Triton said something about my birthday when I first met him, but I didn't really think much of it," I said shaking my head in confusion.

"Well, if that's what you were told, then you have been lied to for absolutely your whole life," Ryder said laughing. "How old did you think you were turning?"

"14. Yeah, well, what else is new?" I leaned against the outer walls of the castle.

"Well, today you actually turn 15. So, what's the plan Topaz?" Ryder whispered.

"Umm, well, I was just gonna wing it," I shrugged.

Ryder stared at me. "Yep, it's definitely me with the brains."

"Ha ha, your such a comedian," I said as I slipped through the open door and cowered in behind a pillar and held my breath.

"Jasper! How could you let her escape?" a deep voice rumbled.

"That's King Erasmus, our Grandfather's friend,"

Ryder explained. "He has four children, all with different mothers, except for Jasper and Cowan who are twins. There's Jasper, Cowan, Jordan, and Jasmine," Ryder whispered beside me.

I nodded and poked my head out carefully from behind the pillar. There stood the brown-haired boy, Jasper. I furrowed my brow. Letting out a sharp gasp I covered my mouth as Ryder pulled me back behind the pillar.

"I'm sorry Father. Cowan tried to pry Sapphire away but went down in the attempt." Jasper bowed his head.

"Like I care about Sapphire! Jasper, Sapphire was Cowan's job. Which Jordan is now fulfilling while you stand in front of me blithering like an idiot. I want no excuses this time young man. Find her! I want Topaz before me by the next sundown! The enchantment won't work otherwise. Now go! Do not stand before me until she is here! I want to have a little talk with that Princess," exclaimed Kind Erasmus.

Ryder gripped my arm harder and I turned to him. He put a finger to his lips. I nodded my head. "Wait until my signal Topaz. When I give the signal, be quiet and go release Dad. Take him to the ship and get Bay to heal him. Do it quickly."

"What's the signal?" I asked a little bit louder than necessary.

"What was that?" King Erasmus' voice boomed.

"It was I, your Majesty," Ryder answered coming out from behind the pillar. "I came to call on thy beautiful daughter, Jordan, my beloved. I am afraid the wedding must be held off. My Grandfather was found nearly dead this afternoon."

"I am deeply sorry for you, my brother." Jasper

came forward, and clapped my brother on the back. I felt so deceived as I saw the fake look of concern that Jasper painted on his face. Jasper, wanted me dead! I believed that he was going to help. I had kissed him, I began to fall in love with him and he just wanted me dead. I narrowed my eyes, clutching a knife in my hand.

"How are your sisters holding up Ryder? I mean, it should be quite hard on poor Sapphire. With your Father gone all these years, your Grandfather raised the two of you. Topaz is only learning she has a family, only to find her Grandfather near deaths doors," Jasper said.

Every word he said felt like a knife to my heart. I never even got to meet my Grandfather. I crumpled to the floor, still making sure I was concealed.

"Topaz isn't very emotional. If she were feeling anything she wouldn't even show it. I would guarantee it," Ryder answered.

I took that as the signal. I got up quickly from sulking in the shadows and went towards the cage. Concealed by a cloud of shadows, I swam as quickly as I could towards my Father.

"T ... Topaz is ... is that you?" My Father was all bent up, struggling over to the bars of the cage. I quickly nodded my head and pressing a finger to my lips he shut his mouth, smiled at me, and then slumped onto the floor of the cage again.

"I'm gonna get you out of here," I whispered. "Just keep quiet."

I stared at the lock, and then closed my eyes. I imagined the water forming the shape of a key, and heard the lock click open. I opened my eyes. The door swung open and I thought I was looking at Ryder but his eyes were different. They were just like mine, and his hair was peppered with grey.

I inched forward into the cage. I knelt over, trying to think of how to do this.

"I'm gonna get you to the surface okay?"

He nodded his head and then it lolled to the side. He was losing strength. I stepped out of the cage as my Dad's face went a little blue and I sunk a little under his weight. I wrapped his one arm around my shoulders and began to swim up hurtling towards the open ceilings of the castle. I looked down at my brother, and almost as if planned, he looked up at me. Ryder nodded to me and I swam even faster to the surface.

I looked slowly over to my Dad. His lips were parted ever so slightly so that little bubbles of air escaped and were rising slowly, upward to the surface. I was going as fast as I could when we broke the surface and I gasped as his weight became even heavier.

There was a ladder hanging down from the side of the boat and I gripped onto it. I closed my eyes and the ladder rose slowly to the deck. I shoved my Father over the edge of the boat and onto the deck. I followed closely behind him.

"Bay, I need you to help my Dad. Quickly, I think he's stopped breathing," I begged as I dragged him a little bit further from the edge of the boat and looked up.

Something hit me across the head, and my vision went black.

Jake

Thomas yelled from beside me, "don't you dare touch her!"

I felt him struggle, elbowing me in the gut.

"Awe, poor baby." Jordan pouted from beside Tamina. She pulled Tamina up by the hair, dragging her along the deck and letting go of her right in front of the two of us. Tamina's head bounced off of the deck and her eyelids fluttered a little bit.

"What's going on?" Tamina asked, blinking a few times and then looked at Thomas and me and then she turned to face Jordan.

"Pamela?" she looked at her quizzically.

"Don't call me Pamela you little worm! You know who I am. I'm not Pamela anymore," Pamela screamed and kicked Tamina in the stomach.

Tamina took the beating and crumbled to the deck, holding her stomach.

"You may have been Princess Topaz at one point," Pamela said leaning over a little bit. "Your Grandfather named me the new Queen while on his death bed. Now get up and fight you little coward"

"He isn't dead yet!" Tamina struggled to get to her feet. Pamela shoved the hilt of a sword into Tamina's hands.

Tamina was immediately in a fighting stance. Pamela looked stunned by her. Pamela, not even thinking, lunged at her. Tamina dodged her with ease and she smirked at Pamela. Pamela lunged again, but as

Tamina dodged her for a second time, Pamela punched her in the stomach.

"Haven't you figured out who I am yet little Tammy? You seem to have a talent for corrupting the minds of boys."

"Your Jordan. Jasper's sister, and you want me dead," Tamina gasped.

"Ah yes, you do have a brain in that oversized fake head of yours."

"The only fake one here Jordan, is you," Tamina said getting back to her feet. "As long as I'm still alive you will never be the Queen."

"Well, isn't that the whole idea, Cupcake?" Jordan smiled smugly at Tamina.

"The creatures of the ocean will never accept you or anyone in your family on the throne. Not after they figure out what you did to us," Tamina snapped at her.

"They don't have to accept what's coming, they will never be able to stop it. Not after you and your sister are dead," Jordan said.

"Your missing one tiny detail Jordan," Tamina hissed, crossing her arms.

"Oh, yes? What's that?" Jordan inquired, amused.

"Ryder's still alive," Tamina said standing as straight and as solid as a wooden beam.

Jordan looked quizzically at Tamina, tilting her head to the side.

"So, what? He loves me; he wouldn't suspect anything of little ol' me. Believe me, he wouldn't even think it could be me who planned the assassination to kill his Grandfather, or his sisters, or his Father even," Jordan mused. "He's too gullible, and too stupid. To think about the little details Topaz, I thought you would've been a little bit smarter too. I have this all planned out and I'm sorry to say, you aren't included in this plan."

Tamina glared at her.

"Jordan. Why are you doing this? We haven't done anything to you or your family to deserve this punishment. Why do you need us all dead?"

"I'm afraid I'll have to leave that to my Father to explain to you," Jordan said a little bit louder than normal, "and when he does come, there'll be hell for you to pay. Enjoy your powers while you still can Topaz, cause when my Father gets here, there mine."

She grinned evilly at Tamina, and then slapped her across the face.

"In the meantime, I'm sure my Father wouldn't mind me softening you up a little bit. He just wants you alive."

Jordan kicked Tamina in the stomach again and she fell backwards collapsing onto the deck, not moving this time and not trying to get up, almost like she had given up.

Jasper

Ryder threw the knife at me. It embedded itself right into the wall, just inches from my head.

"So, Jasper you want us all dead, huh?" Ryder asked, the muscles in his arms bulging.

"No, I don't want you dead Ryder, my Father does," I countered. "I'm just trying to help you. Get out of here now. I know you rescued your Dad. Go now, because in a few minutes the guards will be here and arresting, if not trying to kill you."

Ryder threw another knife. "LIES!"

"LOOK IF YOU WANT TO TEST YOUR LUCK, FINE STAY! IT'S NOT MY FAULT IF YOU GET KILLED STAYING!" I yelled at him.

I stepped away from the wall. "Listen to me Ryder. You have less than 4 minutes. Leave now and help your sisters, please! My brother Cowan tried to get Sapphire killed. He lied to me and said he would protect them both, but he was trying to get them killed. Topaz wasn't there thankfully, but Cowan is now dead! I care about Topaz, and she would never forgive me if you died in our castle, please!"

"You haven't even met Topaz, Jasper. You don't know her," Ryder said.

"Yes, I have. I was supposed to find them and bring them back to the castle, but I couldn't. Topaz was just so beautiful."

"Ewe, Jasper please. Don't tell me your crushing on my sister? Jasper, you haven't seen her when she's angry. I can tell you this, she hates you."

"No. Don't you dare say that to me. The necklace that she wears, it changed color. She cares about me too."

"Not anymore. She heard your little conversation with your Father and I could sense her anger building. Didn't you hear the tides change a little early?" Ryder asked. "When was the last time that happened?"

"When Princess Rhode died," I started.

"Exactly, and you know why the tides changed then, don't you?" Ryder asked pressing on.

"Because when you give birth to twin half-bloods, the power you have to give to their mortal spirit is too immense, and you end up dying in the process," I answered.

"No, that's not even how my Mother died. Why did the tides change?" Ryder pressed on, coming forward and putting a hand on my throat.

"The tides changed because your Mother, Princess Rhode, was in pain?" I offered.

His hand tightened. "No. It changed because Topaz started to cry. Do you know how it changed back only minutes after?" Ryder asked.

"No. I don't know. Do you have a problem with that?"

His hand tightened again, it became harder to breath. "The tide changed back because Sapphire had stopped crying."

"Can you let go of my throat now?" I asked hopefully.

He let go and I dropped to the floor gasping.

"So what? Ryder, we all know those two are powerful."

"Yeah, but you didn't see them today. Your sister, with her huge storms, almost cracked the ship. Sapphire kept the boat from cracking and Topaz helped me keep the water up and out of the ship," Ryder explained.

"We kind of figured it was them," Jasper said.

"Sapphire passed out afterwards. Topaz literally collapsed and then jumped in the water and swam all the way down here, unlocked the cage, grabbed our Father and then rocketed to the surface. I think Sapphire passed as much energy as she could into Topaz, otherwise they both would've just walked away from that attack like it was nothing. I almost passed out."

Tamina

"For 15 years you have been a pain in everyone's butts, now when my Father gets here, you will be free to join your Mother," Jordan smirked and punched me in the gut. My breath left my lungs for a couple of seconds as I was left gasping for its' return.

"Yeah well, if you weren't trying to kill me, I wouldn't be such a pain," I spat. "Why do you want me dead? Wouldn't it be easier to kill me now and take the throne away from us, away from my family?" I asked.

"I'm sorry Topaz, I'll have to let my Father answer that," Jordan answered smirking at me.

"Are you still that much of a follower, Jordan? I can't believe that you are going to kill me, just because your Father told you too."

She glared at me, spat in my face and then shoved me over. I fell onto my left elbow, giving me the feeling that I just got shocked with lightning. I took a sharp intake of breath. I touched the rope that was tied around my wrists. The one end was loose and I pulled it and the knot came free.

"Jordan, stop it! You don't need to hurt her." Thomas struggled against the Devils.

"Thomas you've done enough to me. I don't need your help. I think you've proven just how much you care about me," I snapped at him.

Turning my head slightly, I watched his eyebrows

go up and his eyes looked deep into mine.

Jordan took her hand and squished my face, turning it to look at her. "What have I missed with the perfect couple?" Jordan asked.

"When were we ever a couple?" I spat out.

She raised her eyebrows. She looked at the Devil standing behind me, nodded and then I was wrenched to my feet. All the strength left my arms and legs. I went limp as my muscles in my arms went numb and I felt like falling over.

"You want to know why I want you dead? Fine, I'll tell you. I want you dead because you might be the only person who is better than me. I want to be the only one beautiful enough to change minds, control people's decisions and have every boy fall in love with me with just a single look." She let go of my face, and it took everything in my power to keep myself upright.

"Why don't you just kill me and get it over with? Why do you have to wait for your Father, Jordan?" I interrogated.

"Because, at midnight my Father has to extract your control of the sea from you. From you, Sapphire, Ryder, from everyone in your family. Tonight is the night of your fifteenth birthday. You will officially be of age to accept the throne. You must give both my Father and I your control and you can be free to survive. If you can survive," she smirked at me.

"I will never give you the power voluntarily Jordan, no matter what you do," I gasped as she kicked my stomach. I bent over a little, almost into a bow.

"I'm sorry Topaz, but you have a choice, right now. It's either you give us the power, or we kill you," Jordan said kneeling on one knee. "Your choice."

"Never." I spat.

"Wrong answer," she said.

Ryder

"So, they're more powerful?" Jasper gasped.

I tightened my fist again. "Yes!" I exclaimed.

"Okay, jeez!" Jasper said, regaining breath. "Ryder, I would leave right now."

"Why?" I asked raising my eyebrows.

"The guards are going to walk in, in three, two, one."

On cue, the door burst open and the guards came charging through.

"Jasper, are you okay to swim?" I murmured to him.

He nodded his head a little, rising from the ground.

"Well, then swim!" I yelled.

We propelled ourselves upwards. The guards followed. I swam into a ray of sunshine and the guards shrieked and shrunk back into the shadows. There were two chasing after Jasper.

"Get into the light!" I shouted to him.

He looked over at me quickly and

swam into another sunbeam. The guards responded the same way as the others had a moment before. We started to swim again, being careful to not move from the beams of sun, and we broke the surface of the water.

"Jasper, we need to get up there."

"No, really? Thank you Captain Obvious!"

"Shut up," I glared.

I grabbed ahold of the ladder and started climbing. I came face-to-face with my Father as I reached the top.

"Ryder, Topaz is back! Isn't that ni-ice? I ca-can't believe it. Whe-ere is y-your Mother? She'll be so excited that sh-he is here," he stuttered as is eyes rolled into the back of his head.

I shoved him farther onto the deck and hid him behind a barrel and a ton of rope. I pulled myself up and hid right beside him. I could hear Jordan speaking.

"I'm sorry Topaz you have a choice, right now. It's either you give us the power, or we kill you," Jordan said.

Every word of what Jordan said was like a stab to the heart. I trusted Jordan. I was going to marry her, and she just wanted me for my power. I felt so betrayed.

"Never," Tamina said.

That's my sister! I thought in my head. Just try to break her Jordan, just try to break our family. We can't be broken.

"Wrong answer." I hear Jordan spit.

My heart sinks and I'm scared for Topaz. I've seen how violent Jordan can be, but I've seen how strong Topaz can be. Topaz can't be broken. I can't be broken. Sapphire can't be broken. Eat that Jordan!

Jake

Tamina screamed, jumped to her feet and let the rope drop from her wrists. She grinned at Jordan. Picking up a sword from the ground, Tamina swiftly, and as easy as slicing through bread, slit the throat of the Night Devil that was guarding us. I turned around quickly and took the staff out of its hand. I held it, and walked towards Bay.

"You okay?" I asked.

Bay smiled, "I'm fine now."

I leaned over and kissed her cheek. I watched another Night Devil step up and try to stab Bay. I stuck up the staff and it stopped it midair.

"Can't you see we're trying to have a moment here?" I asked.

Turning the staff around and using the hooked end, I knocked the staff out of its hands and stuck the knife into its chest and turned it before pulling it out.

"I love it when you try to protect me," Bay said smiling, "but now would be the time you need to protect yourself."

She wrapped her arms around me and I leaned in to kiss her. She took a stab with the knife. I gasped thinking it was going to go straight through me, but it went right past me, stabbing a Night Devil that had crept up behind us.

"Like now for instance."

"Thanks," I said.

"No problem." She kissed me softly and then sprinted

off to climb the rope ladder leading up to the crows' nest. I turned and stood right beside Thomas and watched the battle start.

"You ready to fight?" I asked him.

He hesitated a little and then nodded his head. "Yeah, I'm ready."

"Good, cause if you survive this, I think Tamina's gonna kill you."

I lunged forward stabbing one of the Night Devils in the heart and used the staff to knock another off his feet. I jumped up just as the creature swiped the floor hoping to catch me off guard. I landed on its blade, and used my foot to dislodge the staff from his grip. I kicked up the staff with my foot and jumped up. Doing a barrel roll in the air, my foot connected with the wood of the staff and it went flying, lodging itself into the wall. I landed on my feet again and stabbed the struggling creature in the heart.

I looked up quickly to see that Bay and Mallory were standing back to back throwing knives down at us, at the Devils. Bay's throw just missed Jordan's head, clipping off a lock of her hair. It fell to the floor. Jordan screamed. Turning, she chucked a sword up at Bay and Mallory. It came up short, and the sword lodged into the mast just below the crows' nest. Jordan glared up at the nest, stomped off to the rope ladder, and started climbing. I panicked and took the sword and boomeranged it. It went soaring through the air and cut the rope in half, just before Jordan's hand reached up to pull herself higher. Jordan came tumbling down, landing on her back. I saw her struggling to regain her breath, but I left her alone. Jordan had no idea who threw that sword and it was going to stay that way.

I turned back to the fight behind me to see a sword

come down on Thomas, who was lying weaponless on the ground and scrambling backwards. I quickly grabbed another sword from the ground and deflected the Night Devil's sword sending it flying out of the Devil's hands. I pulled my sword up to the Devil's throat and slit it, sending it crashing forward as Thomas rolled off to the side, just avoiding getting squashed.

I offered a hand to Thomas. He gripped it and I helped him to his feet.

"Thanks," he muttered looking at his feet.

"Anytime," I said back smugly. "Not so weak now, am I?"

He shook his head and stood up straight. I was now two inches taller than him. I grew a lot in the days out here.

"No, not really. Can't call you squirt now can I?" Thomas asked.

I shook my head. "Nope, and if you do, I'll kill you."

Tamina

I dropped to the floor, and rolled off to the side. With my arms crossed across my chest, I looked up as a Night Devil brought its' sword down on me. I rolled to the side again, and up onto one knee. I stabbed at it again, but it caught my sword in its hands. I could see the blood pouring from its palms as it pulled back, and I gripped the handle and pulled the sword towards me. It was like a game of tug of war. I twisted the blade and it screamed out. I sent the sword flying through its chest and it coughed a little blood in my face and into my eyes. I closed them and dropped my sword to rub my eyes, trying to get the blood out. My eyes burned.

I opened my eyes and snatched the sword out from his chest. I turned to see Jake helping Thomas up, Jack sticking a sword through a Devil, and Jayden falling to the ground, blood spurting out of his neck with a vacant look in his eyes. I closed my eyes quickly, said a tiny prayer for him and then continued fighting.

I began taking the Devils on four at a time, dodging their blows with swift catlike movements. I felt like a tiger. I was moving so fast I felt as if no one could see me.

A sword came right by my face and I backhanded it away. I put three fingers together and poked the Devil in the gut making it reel forward, and I stabbed a Devil approaching and skewered another bent over. It coughed blood onto my bare feet as I kicked it in the face sending it into a backwards flip. Landing on its neck, I heard the bone snap and I cringed.

A fist came at my face and I caught it just before it hit my nose. I pulled my head back a bit and looked past the fist to see it was another Devil. I groaned.

I forced it back and did a barrel roll in the air kicking it in the face. I could feel blood touch my toes. I landed on one knee, fingers just scraping the wood on the deck with my hair flying all over the place. I heard a gun go off and I quickly dropped to the ground.

I looked up, slowly. Thomas dropped to the floor right beside Jayden. I got to my feet, gripping the knife and sword in both of my hands. Jordan held the gun to her mouth and blew over top of the barrel, clearing it of smoke. She grinned at me.

"Topaz, you shouldn't let people give up their lives for you. This is just between my family and yours," Jordan said sweetly.

I held back the tears burning at the back of my eyes, and then I remembered Thomas hitting me and screaming. I felt sorry I couldn't have forgiven him before this. Now it was too late for that.

"Fine then, just me and you Jordan. May the best girl win!" I said setting myself into a stance.

"Yes, let's go with that Topaz. May the best girl win." She gave me an evil grin. I swallowed.

Jordan took two of the staffs from the ground, left from fallen Devils. They were longer and curved, giving them a greater reach than I had. Jordan was also about half a foot taller than me. She started to run.

"Wait!" Someone shouted.

Jordan stopped and looked around and then dropped to her knees. So did everyone else around me.

"You must be Topaz?" the voice said, as two shadowed figures approached me. One of them was Jasper. I glared at him and stood up straight holding my chin up a little.

"Yes, I am. I go by Tamina though. You must be Jordan's Father?"

He nodded, smiling and showing his yellow teeth. He had salt and pepper hair, and Jaspers' blue eyes.

"Yes, my name is King Erasmus. Future heir to both the bottom and the top of the ocean, making me supreme ruler of the ocean," he said, standing up a little straighter while adjusting his crown.

"Jordan, Jasper, by my side please," King Erasmus commanded.

Jasper stepped up a little bit, and Jordan rose from her bow and stood beside her Father.

"Jordan, where is her twin?" he asked looking to the side slightly but not taking his eyes off me.

"Sapphire is in the weapons room, with Jack sir," Jordan answered slowly.

"Get her."

Jordan left her Father's side and opened the door to the weapons room. Sapphire was being pushed forward. Her face was caked with dried blood and deep cuts covered her face. A long jagged cut stretched from her eyebrow and continued down her face and across her cheek, stopping right at her jawline. She was shoved to the ground right beside me.

I bent down. "Sapphire, are you okay?"

She looked at me, and started sobbing. "Please keep fighting, Topaz. Don't let them win."

"Saph, we are both going to keep fighting, do you hear me. I'm not going to let you die, as long as you don't give up on me," I whispered.

Tears flooded down my face and I suppressed a sob. I stood up again.

"Jasper, now bring forth Ryder," King Erasmus commanded.

Jasper stayed put and looked to his feet.

"Jasper, now!" King Erasmus yelled again. Jasper flinched and turned, nodding to another one of the soldier Devils. Ryder was pushed forward landing at my feet. Both of his eyes were glassy and an empty white. He looked blind.

Jake

Tamina bent forward, leaning overtop of Ryder. Her siblings had been injured so that Tamina would cooperate and I could hear her sobbing.

She rose to her feet, stood up straight, and gave King Erasmus the death stare. I swear if she had laser-vision, he'd be dead, and his ashes obliterated.

"Topaz, there is still ten minutes left. You still have a choice. Give us the power and keep your beautiful face, or have us force the power out of you, and have to lose it. No pressure."

"You know, most times when someone says that, there is always pressure," Tamina spat at him.

"I like the fire in this one." King Erasmus stepped forward a little and set a hand on her shoulder, but quickly pulled his hand away as if he had been shocked.

"She burnt me!"

Jasper and Jordan came forward.

"Land and Ocean. Fire and Ice. Father, we must do the ceremony now, or the power will be fused to their souls and they will live forever," Jordan said quickly.

"Get her on her knees," King Erasmus demanded.

The Devils that had come aboard with the King and Prince surrounded us, gripping our arms to hold us in place. Two Devils came forward and approached Tamina. One forced her arms behind her back, and the other kicked the backs of her knees. She went forward onto her knees. The creature pulled her head back forcing her to look up at the full moon. Sapphire and

Ryder were forced into the same position.

King Erasmus started to speak in a secret language. Jordan began reciting a poem or chant out loud. She unsheathed a long knife with a long white and silver handle that held a diamond-encrusted blade.

"The blood of the taker," Jordan announced, as she slit her forearm.

"The blood of the givers," she announced, as she took the blade and cut Tamina in a diagonal line, starting at her neckline and ending just above the first button on her white blouse. Jordan did the same thing to Ryder and Sapphire.

"The blood of the accepter." King Erasmus held out his forearm and Jordan slit it also. She gathered some of each of their blood into a small glass vial.

"Fire and Ice, Topaz and Sapphire. The Land and Ocean twins, voluntarily give up their powers of control over the ocean to King Erasmus, and all of his heirs." Jordan waved her arms and poured the mixed blood over King Erasmus' head. Streaks of the blood poured down onto his face, turning his eyes red.

"Do you accept King Erasmus?" she asked.

"Yes. I accept the burden of the changing tides, the storms, the fate of the ocean," answered King Erasmus.

I watched Tamina's stone-faced expression change as she screamed in agony, just as King Erasmus also began to scream as his skin bubbled over his face, neck and arms. Sapphire's head went limp, and Ryder fell forward onto the deck.

Everything and everyone went quiet.

"Did it work?" King Erasmus asked breathlessly, breaking the uneasy silence. Jordan shrugged her shoulders.

"Get her to her feet! We'll settle this permanently. The ocean now belongs to me," King Erasmus shouted as his face turned the exact shade of a ripe tomato.

Tamina

The agony was fake. I don't know if King Erasmus' was, but mine was.

I was pulled to my feet and all of my energy was forced out of me, trying to keep Ryder and Sapphire alive. It was all over.

King Erasmus came towards me, holding that beautiful yet deadly knife. He knelt on one knee. "Looks like you are going to lose your beautiful face, but not in the way you expected huh?"

"I was always expecting this Erasmus. I knew it was going to happen," I said looking up at him, tears shone in my eyes. "I'll never forgive you for this, and neither will the ocean.

His eyes glittered. "Are you sure?" he asked.

"Absolutely positive," I glared at him. I looked past him, at Jasper. I glared at him. King Erasmus followed my eyes.

"Ah, so you have met my other son."

"Father, just get it over with," Jasper gasped, clenching his fists at his sides.

"Remember what I said boy," King Erasmus said, as he got up and shoved the knife into Jasper's hand.

"Do it, kill her Jasper!" King Erasmus ordered.

Jordan put herself in between her Father and her brother. "I'll do it Father, let me kill her. I am not as weak as Jasper."

King Erasmus shoved her aside. "You've done

enough Jordan," he said as Jordan tumbled to the ground. Jordan got to her feet, and went behind a pack of barrels. She emerged a moment later dragging a body. Jordan sat behind her Father and brother, raised a knife to my father's throat, and slit it.

I breathed deeply, tears welled in my eyes and stung as I held them back. All I could think of while my throat constricted, and as I stifled a sob was goodbye.

Jasper

My Father pressed the knife into my hands. "Don't be soft boy," he whispered to me. "Just kill her and the whole ocean will be in our hands."

I looked at Topaz and she looked drained. Tired. Exhausted. I immediately felt my heart sink in my chest. I walked over to her and got down on my knees. I traced her face with my hand as she turned her head away from me. Ryder was right, she hated me.

"I'm sorry," I mouthed.

"I don't care," she mouthed back. "You played me like a card."

I shook my head. "No, I didn't. I didn't know this was going to happen."

"Don't try to apologize to me."

I took a deep breath and leaned over and pressed my lips against hers but she pushed me away. I closed my eyes and felt my heart in my stomach as I stood up again.

"I really am sorry this is happening Topaz," I stated, hoping she'd turn and look at me. She did look up, but glared at me. Through her beautiful dark grey eyes, I could see her holding something back. Sorrow, love, pain, tears?

I felt dead. I raised the knife in both of my hands, keeping my eyes on her face. She let her eyelids fall over her eyes as tears flowed down her cheeks. She didn't sob, she just let the tears fall down her face, leaving tiny streaks of water leading down her cheeks and over the corners of her mouth, which was turned down into a frown.

I crumbled to my knees again and let the knife fall out of my hands, it skidded across the wood, and stopped right at Jordan's feet. She bent over, picked it up, and came charging towards us.

Tamina

I kept my eyes closed. I didn't want to see his face when he killed me. Although, I was already dead on the inside.

I was sprayed with someone's spit. Then, Jordan whispered in my ear, "this is it, Topaz. No matter what you do, you are going to be one of the last Jackson's. How does it feel?"

I opened my eyes slightly, looking at her through my eyelashes. I mustered up all the saliva I could and spat in her face.

She exhaled exasperated. "Not good then," her eyes twinkled.

I lifted my head to the sky. The stars were going to be the last thing I saw before I died. I listened to Jordan rise to her feet, and start to chant a war cry. I understood it, just as I had understood King Erasmus' earlier chants.

'Heart of a Lion, blood of the ocean, die now, in your own blood, for you belong no where but in Hell."

I blinked a little. Jordan cried out as I kept my eyes to the sky. The sword entered my chest. I tasted blood come to my mouth then dribble over my lips. I gasped for breath, and in that gasp I swallowed some blood, forcing me to cough.

"Dispose of her," Jordan said kicking me over.

I coughed again, and my eyelids closed.

I focused my energy to Sapphire and I felt my

fingertips tingle with the shock of electricity. I kept telling myself I was ready to die. All of my energy was gone. I couldn't give her anything else. I felt my arms go numb as they dragged my body to the edge of the rail, where there was a space from the plank.

"Bye, bye Topaz. Have fun wherever you're going," Jordan whispered to me.

There was a sharp pain in my stomach and then I was falling. I was ready to die. I kept repeating this in my head

"Topaz!"

My name was the last thing I heard as I tumbled into the ocean. I was ready to die. That was the last thought in my mind as my world went dark.

Jasper

I felt the small tears fall down my face as I watched Topaz fall to the ocean. I couldn't help it. She was dead! I screamed her name again, and my body went rigid. I melted to my knees. She was gone. Nothing could stop my Father now. What I had done? If the ceremony worked at least.

I looked back at everyone. They were glowing a bright yellow, and not paying any attention to me. I took a deep breath and threw myself overboard, executed a perfect dive into the water. This water knew me. I let it carry me down until I saw her. I watched her sink slowly and calmly through the water. I couldn't let her sink to the bottom.

I raced towards Topaz, but the water was now fighting me, like it had figured out what I had done, what my family had done, and thought I was going to hurt her.

Her hair spun away from her face, weaving itself into a wreath around her head. Her eyelashes moved with the current and her lips, now a pale blue, moving, changing into a light purple. Her lips parted slightly allowing little bubbles to escape her mouth. I quickly counted the seconds between bubbles, 23 seconds. Her skin was a color lighter than porcelain and she sank further and further into the oceans depths.

This was the girl my family wanted dead. This was

the girl who had her life ruined, her family torn apart, because of my family's greed. This was the girl I had fallen in love with, the girl that I wanted to live, and I was going to help her. She was Topaz, the Ocean Princess! Either I throw everything away letting her die, or I save her!

I wrapped my arms around her waist, pulling her closer to me. I felt like a torpedo, soaring towards the surface of the water. My face broke the seal of the water and I breathed in air. My tail treading enough water to keep both of us afloat. I pressed her against the rope ladder, looping her arms on the rungs. I touched my hand to the hole in her chest, closed my eyes and felt the water rushing through my fingers. I smelt her blood on my hands. Underneath the touch of my fingers the hole filled, and her wound healed. I opened my eyes again, and I saw Topaz's eyelids flutter.

I smiled at her.

"Wh-what happened?" she asked.

I took her face in my hands and pulled her towards me and I kissed her. She wrapped her arms tightly around my neck.

"You saved me?" she asked. "How did you do it?"

"Well, let's say that the vial of blood was incomplete."

"What?"

"Jordan was supposed to take my blood also and put it in the vial. I left that part out when I gave her the ritual. Jordan was also missing the line which stated that the greedy would die."

"You have the power?" she asked me.

"Yes, and no. I have your sister's power. You still have yours," I said.

She looked at me again. Right at me, like she was searching for something, something to trust.

"How do I know I can trust you?" she whimpered.

"I just saved your life. I think that's enough, but if not, it's at least a straw to grasp at." I smiled.

She grinned back at me, and pulled me closer to her. I buried my face in her hair.

"We're in this together now. You hear me?" I whispered in her ear.

"Yes," she whispered back as she pulled away from me and kissed my cheek. "Thank you."

Tamina

He came back for me!

I swam out a little bit, with thoughts of Jasper running through my mind. I took a deep breath and leaned back into the water on my back. Floating on my back, I closed my eyes, and let the water engulf me in its iron grip, covering me head to toe with its waves. Suddenly I was moving, and I let my arms control the ocean again. I opened my eyes and found that I was in a thundering wave, rising above the ship. King Erasmus was lying dead on the deck, and Jordan was glowing a bright, bright yellow. She looked up at me scared.

The ocean formed a bridge, not touching the deck but ending a foot above it. I left the water bridge and stepping onto the deck, I picked up the white knife abandoned on the ground.

"Jordan, how about we end this our way?" I offered. "A fight to the death. Just you and me."

"Fine," she snapped. "I have the power of the ocean now, you don't."

"Whatever you say Jordan," I rolled my eyes.

I got into a stance with my weight on the balls of my feet. The knife fit perfectly in my hand, weighing evenly on both ends. It felt like it was made for me. I took a deep breath in, and exhaled. I was ready for her first attack and I studied her movements. I could tell that she was placing all of her weight on her left leg, and that her right foot hovered over the floor. She was using her right hand for the sword, as her left forearm was bleeding heavily.

She lunged again and I stuck my knife in front of my face to meet her sword. Using it to push off, I spun on my right foot like a ballerina. Slicing my knife through the air again, she stuck her left hand out to block the blade. The knife easily sliced through her palm, as she howled in agony.

I shoved her, and she stumbled backwards. I let her catch her balance, and set her stance again. I put my knife out, my left hand behind my back. She clenched her teeth, and narrowed her eyes at me. She didn't scare me at all.

Jordan lunged again and dropped to the ground, sliding over the wood on her knees, her sword cutting rigidly through my side. I screamed in pain. My free hand flew to my cut and I could feel the blood gushing as the scent of it filled the air around me.

I staggered a little bit, but kept on my feet. I tried to keep my weight balanced on both of my legs. The blood rolled through the cracks in between my fingers, making my hand sticky and warm. I took a deep breath in through my nose and then exhaled out my mouth. I paused, closed my eyes and waited. It was around two in the morning, one of the darkest hours of the night. From experience, I'd say that this was when I fought best. I kept my eyes squeezed shut and just listened. I heard the wood creak under someone's feet. It was coming from my left. I swung my knife in that direction and it clanged against another knife as the owner's strength forced me back.

I smiled despite myself. Jordan didn't know me

at all! The weight of the sword disappeared and I heard the ring of metal in the air. The blade swept along the floor, whistling through the air as I hopped over it. I heard another frustrated grunt and I opened my eyes again.

Jordan was glowing brighter and brighter, but she also looked like she was wasting away. She swung her sword but it seemed heavy in her hands, and her movements were becoming sluggish.

I spun around, pirouetting again on my left foot. My right side burned and felt even hotter than I expected a devils armpit to feel like. My blade crashed with hers and I put my other hand on my knives hilt. I pushed forward with all of my might. I clenched my teeth, and my arms began to scream with the force I was pushing against.

Jordan muttered something. I caught the words just before the wind took them away, "I hope you die a painful death Topaz."

I laughed, pushing even harder than before and watched her fall backwards. In a quick movement I brought the blade down on her cheek. It carved her skin perfectly, matching the cut on my cheek. I did the same with her other cheek. Then suddenly the cut on my neck started to burn, as if it was reminding me not to forget about it too.

I spoke in our language, "I'm not going to die Jordan. You are." Then I carved the same diagonal line into Jordan's neckline, and the burning I felt subsided.

I let Jordan get to her feet, but she stumbled a bit. I slashed at her shin and cut through her skin easily and she went down again.

"What's happening to me?" she asked.

"You could never have the power I have."

Jordan's eyebrows knit together in confusion. "What do you mean? Of course I have power. How else would I have been able to defeat you?" she questioned.

"I mean, you said the incantation wrong, and you didn't include Jasper's blood. You didn't get it right. You never defeated me," I answered.

"I have power you will never have, no matter how much you deny it! Live with it Topaz, I'm stronger than you!" Jordan argued.

I smiled and shook my head. "Power? You never had it."

I raised my white knife and it started to grow in size. The blade growing longer, and beginning to bend, making itself into a sort of claw or a talon.

She spoke in English to me. "Please, please Topaz. You're better than this. You can't kill people. It'll kill you on the inside. Please, save me! It burns!"

I dropped my arms. I glared at her, and then my eyes relaxed and I raised my eyebrows.

Jordan began to glow so bright. My eyes burned, but I kept looking at her as she began to shin brighter, and brighter. I could see the agony in her expression and there was nothing I could do except end her misery. I raised the knife again and swiftly drove it right through her heart. Going down with the sword, I stopped in a kneeling position.

The bright light dissipated, and along with it, her body also disappeared.

I could hear her thank me through the wind, for ending her pain. Jordan's spirit formed in front of me and she was holding Thomas' hand. I could see her innocence again. She once again looked like Pamela. Jayden came forward along with Blake and Mallory, almost as if they were back from the dead. They grinned at me and then faded away. I reached my free hand out to them, but by the time my hand was almost touching theirs, my hand just fell through mist. I let it drop back to my side.

I took a deep breath. In and out.

I let go of the knife then decided better of it. I jerked out the sword that was buried deep into the wooden planks of the deck. I dropped the knife beside me on the deck floor so that it was close by if I needed it, and then sat down. I brought my knees up to my chest, rested my head on my knees, and began taking long, deep breaths.

Jordan was right; this was going to kill me from the inside.

Jake

I watched Jasper walk over to Tamina, sit down beside her, and wrap his arms around her. She set her head on his shoulder and closed her eyes. They almost seemed frozen in time.

When the spirits of the fallen disappeared, I looked around for Bay and saw her leaning against the wall of the Captain's cabin with her arms crossed. I grinned. She had braided her long brown hair into two braids. Her eyes were shining, but her face looked grim. Something was wrong.

I walked over to her and set my hand on her shoulder. "What's wrong Bay?"

She shook her head, "I don't understand anything, why didn't Tamina die? Why didn't the power transferring thingy work? How are we still alive?"

I grabbed her hand, looked her in the eyes, and leaned forward and kissed her.

"I'm sure we're not the only ones with questions right now. Tamina's probably just as confused as we are. When the time is right, I bet she'll try her best to answer all of our questions. Right now, I'm going to enjoy just being ALIVE." I winked at her.

She shook her head and laughed. "Guess it is awesome, being alive I mean ... what do you think it's like being dead?"

Bay looked away from me, like she was lost in space and trying to crack a puzzle.

"Tamina would know," I stated.

"Yeah, but she probably won't want to talk about it," she countered.

"She probably would," I pointed out.

"She wouldn't, but I'm not that insensitive to ask," she argued.

"Are we really going to argue about this?" I laughed.

She glowered at me. "Yes, and believe me, I don't plan on losing this argument."

I studied her. "What has Tamina done to you?"

Bay looked away from me, let go of my hand and started to walk away. She was about ten feet away when she turned back, smiled at me and said, "she made me stronger. She made me brave."

I grinned at her. No, I thought in my head, you were already this strong; you just didn't know it yet. I ran to catch up with her. I swept her hand up in mine, and our fingers locked.

Tamina

I moved Jasper's arms from around me and stood up. I still gripped the white knife in my hand. Walking over to my siblings, I set it down by their heads.

I kept Sapphire alive for as long as I could, and then she finally began to restore her own energy. I believe Jasper had something to do with that. She sat up a little, the color slowly returning to her face. Her grey eyes shone in the moon, glittering as she gave me a small smile.

"How you feeling sis?" I asked quietly.

She winced and I could tell she was getting dizzy as her eyes glazed over a little.

"Better. I'm sorry I tried to get away. They kept a hold of me and they drained me of my power. I can't control anything anymore, at least not like I used to. Whatever power they got from me, died with them. Now, only the Ocean Princess, that's you Topaz, has any power."

I shook my head, and crossed my legs. "No, it's not your fault. The power didn't die with them. They never had an ounce of the Land power. I promise."

Her eyebrows knit together, "what do you mean?"

"I mean they could never withstand the force of your power. Jasper has it now. He promised me that if you want it back, there is another ceremony we can preform to return your powers to you."

"No! I don't want it. I think I like being a mortal right now. If it's okay with you, I'd like to take your place on land?" She winked at me.

I grinned. "Sure, whatever you want Saph."

I turned my head to look at Ryder. His eyes were glazed over and they were an empty white. At some point during that whole fight between Jordan and I, Ryder had seized breathing, and his heart had failed him.

I closed my eyes and let silent tears roll down my cheeks. I opened them again. Leaning over him I struggled to see through them with the amount of water gathering in my eyes. I pressed my fingers to Ryder's eyelids, and closed his eyes. Now he didn't look dead, he just looked like he was dreaming a peaceful dream and was in the middle of a happy ending.

I smiled a little. Letting a small tear fall from my face and land on his cheek. It began to roll down his cheek to his ear, and it gave me the thought that he looked like he was crying.

I got to my feet, slipped the knife in my belt, and helped Sapphire to her feet. I made sure she could walk on her own as I quickly made my way over to the rail. I set my hands down on the wooden handrail and my nails dug into the wood, scraping off little flakes of it.

An enormous breeze drifted by, I closed my eyes and let it run through my hair, like fingers. Gooseflesh sprouted over my forearms where my blouse didn't cover. I opened my eyes again and I saw my Father standing in front of me, holding hands with a woman, who looked just like me. It must have been my Mother. Then a woman came forward and grinned at me. Aunt Bea. Then, last to join the circle was Ryder.

My Grandfather, Poseidon, came out of the water and he grasped my hand. I fought the urge to run at everyone and engulf them in my arms, but I knew by their glittery sheen and drained colors, that they were only spirits. Just spirits, they weren't really there.

I took a deep and shaky breath and gave a small smile. My Mother held out her hand to me. I reached out to grab it, but my hand went right through hers. I swallowed hard.

"Topaz darling, you were amazing." She praised me. I smiled.

"I am so proud of you Topaz, you listened to your fate. You showed such bravery, for such a young girl," Aunt Bea said as she smiled at me. She wasn't as harsh speaking now and her voice wasn't like metal anymore. It was wispy like a spider web when you walk through it.

"You will make a fine Queen, if you take the role." My Grandfather beamed at me. I blushed and ducked my head in a small bow.

"Princess Topaz, so much for being an innocent bystander, huh?" my Father asked as a mischievous smile played across his lips. His eyes lit up briefly, then his face seemed to remember that he was dead, and the gleam disappeared. "Your just like your Mother."

He squeezed Mother's hand and she looked up at him, love shining in her eyes.

"Topaz it looks like you're the next in line for Queen. Sapphire's crazy for wanting to go to land! Don't worry; we'll be with you every step of the way. You little rebel!" Ryder said putting his hand up for a high-five, then quickly lowering it. He looked at his hand, shook it and then stuck it in his pocket, realizing that as a spirit, he couldn't give a high-five. Tears sprung to my eyes.

"I never got to meet you Mom, what am I supposed to do?" My lower lip quivered.

She made a hushing noise in her mouth, smiled and set a ghostly hand on my shoulder making me shudder. "Do what you think is best. I know you have our Kingdom's best interests at heart. Be the change you want to see in the world."

My Father laughed. "Rhode, did you just quote Gandhi?"

Mother laughed again, "Yes, yes I did. Is that so hard to believe?" She punched him playfully on the shoulder.

I smiled again. My Father nodded his head. "Well, you did live under the ocean. I didn't know you knew of Gandhi."

"Just because I'm a mermaid doesn't mean that I'm as stupid as the rest!" she said defiantly.

"You are such a rebel, sis! Can't wait to see your coronation!" Ryder exclaimed, not being able to wrap his head around what I had done.

"Now hold on a minute Ryder, she hasn't even accepted the role. She may pass on the role of Queen to someone else." My Grandfather's face became serious.

I looked back at my peers and they were all staring at me. I looked to everyone. I led them here and we won the battle for the power over the Ocean. I wonder what I could do with a whole Kingdom behind me.

Jasper winked at me, and nodded his head. I tilted my head to its side as he shrugged his shoulders as if to say, 'Just do it.'

My Grandfather cleared his throat. "Do you accept the role Topaz?"

It was almost as if the whole world were holding it's breath, waiting for my answer. Triton came forward and rested a hand on my shoulder.

Visions of the past few days ran through my mind. Night Devils murdered some of my family and friends, and my whole life had been flipped upside down. I pondered Miss. Cove's words and realized that this was what she meant when she said that I was responsible for learning my own destiny. This is who I was meant to be.

I turned to my Grandfather and announced, "I accept. I will be your Queen of the Seas."

Acknowledgements

I'd like to thank my best friends who kept pushing me to finish this project.

I am grateful to my family, for believing in me and for helping me through my writer's block.

Thank you Bryson, for playing Call of Duty; Black Ops in some of my deepest writing sessions, inspiring most of my battle scenes, and for providing me with a wicked video game soundtrack.

Dad, thanks for providing me with such great music to listen to while in the midst of my writing.

Mom, thanks for standing by me when I needed the help, and understanding exactly what I meant when I couldn't put the words to paper.

I'd also like to thank my grade 6 teacher, Mr. Woodley, for offering to read my rough draft (it was a rough one) and giving me great ideas to improve my book — "Tenses!!"

Lastly, I would like to thank those who continually asked me when my book was going to be finished. If you hadn't shown such a great interest in my writing, I may have abandoned it. You know who you are!

Hope you all stick around for my next novel.

On that happy note, I'd just like to say; never give up, all you need is Faith, Trust, and Pixie Dust!

Read on for a sneak peak of Rylee Loucks' next book

The Children

Chapter

1

prologue

On May 1st 2030, a new species was brought into the world. They were called, The Children. In total, there were 15. Though they reproduced very fast, which no one thought was possible, and the world almost ended. They were stopped.

On January 10th 2040: The Children were kept in a secret compound in Antarctica, called FroZone. FroZone had the world's greatest scientists in the world, working on controlling, and taming this new race.

On this exact date, January 10th 2040, I was born. Yes, me. Cleopatra Jean Tyler, born to Leona and Marcus Tyler who were genius scientists.

4 months later, my best friends Dante and Vanchensa Deluca were born. Two more great minds to add to the list.

Throughout the years of 2040 to 2045, 84 babies were born to the scientists.

The 85th was unexpected.

I was the oldest, and we lived with the greatest minds in the world. So naturally, being our parents, they loved us no matter how dumb we turned out to be, right? Wrong. 5% of us died within the first two months of life. 15% died due to birth defects that killed them within four days. That left 80%, and if your up on your Math, that's 68 scientists' kids.

Now, wait until I get to the good part. If by the time we were 2 years old, and considered of good and sound mind, we were allowed to stay. 28% were then sold off to the world as slaves, and yes, we went back to slavery.

49 of us are left, and now I'm just picking them off one by one. At age three we all started training. I like to refer to it as mental torture, but it depends on how you roll the dice. Training mainly consisted of fighting, handling weapons, and in extreme cases you were sent into an apprenticeship with Assassins. Lucky me, I was the one who got an apprenticeship. I was the only one, who got an apprenticeship. Which meant that I had a weakness for sharp and shiny things, and I could use them without even thinking about it.

Now, on with the executions. Out of that 49, 20 of us were executed for lack of skill in training. If you couldn't handle a knife, you went through each of the weapons. If nothing suited you, you went to hand-to-hand combat. If you couldn't kill someone, well, they killed you.

29 people, and if you're falling behind, well don't be surprised if you hear a knock on your door.

2046: baby number 85 is welcomed into the world.

Her name: Star Tyler, born three weeks late, and completely healthy. She was born exactly 8 days and 6 years after me, and was my little sister. It wasn't odd to have two children, but due to the poor survival rate, it was very rare.

That makes 30 kids.

Life in FroZone went unchanged for another eight years. Before I turned 14 was when things really started to change. All of us survivors had to have a chip implanted in our brain. Only five people knew exactly why. Two weeks after the chip was implanted, those five people were murdered, and The Children escaped.

I am now 14, and lucky you. You've survived the past, lets see if you can handle the present.

CPSIA information can be obtained at www.ICGtesting.com
Printed in the USA
LVOW070800281012

304649LV00005B/17/P